THE TENNESSEE WALTZ

Books by Alan Cheuse:

Candace and Other Stories
The Bohemians
The Grandmothers' Club
Fall Out of Heaven
The Tennessee Waltz and Other Stories

THE TENNESSEE
WALTZ
AND OTHER STORIES
ALAN CHEUSE

PEREGRINE SMITH BOOKS
SALT LAKE CITY

First Edition

95 94 93 92 91 5 4 3 2 1

Copyright © 1990 by Alan Cheuse

This is a Peregrine Smith Book, published
by Gibbs Smith, Publisher, P.O. Box 667,
Layton, UT 84041

Design by J. Scott Knudsen, Park City, Utah

Cover illustration: *The Sources of Country
Music,* by Thomas Hart Benton, courtesy of
the Country Music Foundation, Nashville, TN

Manufactured in the United States of
America

**Library of Congress Cataloging-in-
Publication Data**
Cheuse, Alan.
    The Tennessee Waltz / Alan Cheuse.
        p.   cm.
    ISBN 0-87905-366-6
    I. Title.
PS3553.H436T46   1990
813'.54—dc20   89-29094
                                                      CIP

The paper used in this publication meets
the minimum requirements of American
National Standard for Information
Sciences—Permanence of Paper for Printed
Library Materials, ANSI Z39.48-1984 ∞

For George and Susan Garrett

Contents

Acknowledgments

Grateful acknowledgement is made to the following publications in which stories originally appeared:

"Slides" in *Barbaric Yawp*

"Sources of Country Music" and "The Tennessee Waltz" in *Quarterly West*

"Fishing for Coyotes" in *The New Yorker*

"The Pac-Man Murders" in *Blue Ox Review*

"Garden of the Gods" and "The Quest for Ambrose Bierce" in *Black Warrior Review*

"On the Tram" in *The Bennington Review*

"The Accident" in *Sandlapper*

"Toward Easter Island" in *Real Fiction*

"Land of Cotton" in *Pencil Press Quarterly*

"Nights on the Cumberland Plateau" in *The Texas Review*

"Fishing for Coyotes," "The Quest for Ambrose Bierce," and "The Call" in *Candace and Other Stories,* Apple-wood Books, 1980

THE TENNESSEE WALTZ

SLIDES

Hello! From all the way on the other side of . . .

(Rumble of airplane or truck drowns out the voice)

Hello! I'll try again, Hello! From all the way on the other side of the country where, as you can see—if you've got the first picture up on the carrousel—and *hear,* we're digging out from our monster storm, this is your on-the-spot reporter, your loving Angie . . .

(Rush of air, rumble of voices, high-pitched, barking of dog)

And David, this is your on-the-spot grandson David . . .

(High-pitched shrieks)

David, don't just grab . . .

(Flutter of voices, shrieks, whines)

Okay, Muffin, you can say hello. David, let go. Muffin, here. Folks, this is Muffin . . .

Huhwoah, Gwammie, Huhwoah, Gwam . . .

(Rush of air, shouts)

David! Folks, I'm going to turn off the tape machine for a minute and sort out this mess here. Everybody has to take . . .

Still there? Still on slide one, I hope. As you can see, we're standing in front of the house, and, like I told you when I called, we had no damage at all.

(Muffled sound of child's voice)

Except it was scary, David wants to tell you. David?

It *was* scary, folks, when the tree fell right across the back patio . . .

Thank you, David.

(Children's voices)

Muffin, did you think it was a big storm? Tell your grandparents.

I was fwightened. I cwied for my papa.

(Blast of static)

David . . .

(Sound fades, then picks up with slightly more intense whine and hiss)

Sorry folks. Please go to slide two. (Pause) Here's the famous tree, a little bitty branch off one of the eucalyptus giants that stand around the house, that's all. Not like the big redwoods that came down in the mountains and floated along the river and put out the main bridge. And if it looks a little out of focus like I'd gone cross-eyed or something? That's because famous grandson David here is taking his first picture. Isn't that right, David?

Famous David here, on the scene, in the back patio of the Johnson house. Well, Mama? What do I call it?

(Pause—hiss of tape)

Notice my haircut, folks, which you couldn't really notice all that much in the first slide because of the angle. I'd just had it trimmed in the back then . . .

(Rumble, static)

David! I'll talk. He wants me to tell you that the house isn't called . . . that's the way, just don't touch the knob . . . that I've decided to take back our family name . . . he's just a little confused about it. I suppose I am, too. Please go to slide three.

Here . . . here you can really see my hair. Hope you like it. Remember how you-all used to go on at me for not cutting it? Here . . . and behind me . . . you can see our neighbor's house, they are the Bentons, very nice people, an older couple, sort of an uncle and aunt to us, when . . . the children's father left? They were real nice to us all, those of us left here, I mean. And here's me again, of course, and Muffin playing with her new puppy, . . . yes, dear, if you can get puppy to talk. . . . (Pause) David taking that picture, too. Now to slide four. (Pause) Muffin and puppy again, and David fiddling with his Space Invaders cap. There's a real nice fellow lives in an apartment behind the Bentons's house, they rent to him, and he's a gardener and goes to the university part-time? His name is Robby Ward, and he's been taking David down to the gameroom down in Santa Cruz some afternoons, in fact, the day of the storm they were down there, and came back so drenched you wouldn't have believed it; when the rain started it just seemed like a whole lot of nothing, but then it kept on coming down and coming down . . . You want to put the next slide on? I didn't make a lot of them 'cause they're so expensive but it's cheaper than you-all flying out here right away to see how we're doing, especially with your heart problem, Daddy . . . Yes, Muffin, here you can say it.

I hope you feelin' better, Gwanpa.

David? David come and talk if you're going to talk!

Hope you're feeling better, Granpa.

(Rush of muffled air, whine of tape)

Now you kids go on outside and say hello to Mrs. Benton so Mama can say some grown-up things to your grandparents. (Pause. Change of pitch in tape) Put on slide four now, folks.

Here's me again. I sure hope you like that haircut. Doesn't it put me right back in high school? I wanted to feel like a fresh start after . . . our problem. After the children's father left. (Pause) I don't know why I don't want to say his name but I sure don't. (Pause) Now you asked when you called when the storm was going on were we okay, and I wanted to show you some of the things that went on. So that neighbor of ours, Robby Ward? He took me around with the camera one afternoon just after the rain stopped, when our power was still out. We couldn't get to all the places we wanted to see, a lot of the roads were still out. But here's—turn to the next slide—here's some of it, here's a real tree that fell down, this huge redwood, the earth just washed out from under it, and it slid down the hill maybe a quarter of a mile from our house and you can see it's blocking the road, what road there's left under it.

Slide . . . next slide.

Well, we drove around another way to where we heard an entire subdivision had been washed away. Our power was out—you know we were so lucky to still have the telephone working so that you could call in because it really would have been a tragedy if you couldn't have found out about us, I mean, you just sitting there on the other side of the country not knowing whether we were dead or alive, and I don't know what I would have done if you hadn't called; nobody else called, if you know what I mean (Pause. Tape whirs loudly, then subsides).

This subdivision, the one that washed away, you read about it in the newspapers, I'm sure—didn't you say that the *Daily Journal* was running stories all the time about California, not just big disaster stories. So, it's called, would you believe it? Love Creek? *Love* Creek. And all these people just got washed away in their homes when the mud came down on top of them. This is the place. Looks like a scar on the land, doesn't it? And isn't it just like that terrible thing going on with chemical waste up in New York State? Love Canal? *Love* Canal? How is it these places with names that ought to bring cheer and happiness to people seem to bring these disasters? Well, I know, not always, not always. Well, so here is another shot—next slide please—where you can see part of a roof poking out of the mud. Since then you know they've dug these poor people out, almost a dozen of them here, and buried in the mud doing just what they happened to be doing when the slide came down on them, like the famous old Eye-talian disaster, Robby tells me, the place where Mount Vesuvius erupted way back when in Roman times and the whole town was buried where it stood, or was sleeping, which was what happened here . . . Excuse me, I've got to turn over the tape. So you change the slide and turn it over. (Pause)

There. More disaster. Sorry. But this is your daughter reporter from this side giving you the sad news because you asked for it. More of Love Creek. Since then they dug up one poor man who was talking on the telephone when the mud came down, he was found holding the receiver to his ear. Can you believe that? And who could he have been talking to? Maybe his wife and children who maybe, lucky for them, had gone on a visit to relatives somewhere when the storm hit and wanted to know how things were? Can you imagine what they felt, the line just going dead? Of course, they couldn't have known much except that the power went out. And he, poor soul, he just didn't know anything. Maybe he heard a rumbling sound. And then he looked around. And then it was all over. (Pause) There was *one* story in the paper here, that was sort of comical about one man who said he was sitting in his house up around here listening to the rain and then he heard a loud knock at his back door? So he gets up to answer it, and he opens the door, and it's his guest house, he says, it's his *guest house* just slid down the mountain, and the next thing he knows his own house caves in around him, and the only thing that saved him is that the beams fell down around him in sort of an Indian teepeelike shape and that kept the rest of the house from falling on him and crushing him? Next slide.

More trees down here. All around where the subdivision slid down under the weight of the mud from above. Mama, Dad, I tell you, I felt just like a little girl again, all lost and afraid when we looked around here—you can see we couldn't get too close, the civil defense and the Red Cross was still in there, digging around, and the sheriff's department, state police, state disaster crews, you name it, but can you imagine, they found a couple just buried right in their bed where they were sleeping; they say they were sleeping, but who knows? I don't want to embarrass you with this kind of talk, but think of it a minute, think if they were loving each other at the instant that the mud slid down on their house. Who knows what they could have been feeling? But maybe they were just asleep, and that would have been most merciful, wouldn't it?

Next slide.

Here's a house on the other side of our road, and you can see where the creek is running right through it. See, it split the house right in two. Talk about a break-up! I know, I know what you're thinking, I shouldn't make jokes about a disaster like this, but no one was hurt in this house in the slide . . .

Next one.

Here was a terrible thing. A woman sitting on her sofa watching television with two male friends, now I don't know whether or not she was married to one of them or they were relatives by blood or just friends or what, the newspaper didn't say, and this was too far away from our road to know anyone who could tell us exactly who they were, but she was sitting there, and the mud came through the house they said roaring like a freight train, and the next thing she knows the two men are gone, just rushed away by the mud, and she is still sitting there . . . (Pause)

I'll bet you need some smiles after that one. I know I did. But there wasn't much to smile about up here for days and days. You can change the slide now. Here's a shot of the inn, a fancy place just up the road from us that had a real brook running through the middle of the dining room— that's the kind of thing they do out here, you know? Well, when the rains didn't stop coming, that brook became a river and tore up the whole place, and now they're saying that they just can't imagine ever opening up again there was so much damage, and who knows when the brook will turn into another river? I took this picture. There's Robby, just off to one side—see, he's got that long pigtail. Well, I took the picture because I thought you needed some smiles and that a man wearing a pigtail would make you grin. But he's a wonderful fellow—now don't get any ideas, he's a nice, nice boy, and a good neighbor, and, like I told you, good to David—so. And then there was another happy story, another we heard of up here, where this woman was standing in her house when the mud came through and it pushed her out her window—she broke right through the window and it knocked her unconscious? But the next thing she knows she's sitting in the streambed about a mile from her house, and she's holding onto a big statue, one of those that comes out of the shrines the Catholic people put up in their yards? And she's not a Catholic, and never had been, and she didn't even know any neighbors put up one of those shrines, but she's sitting there holding the thing in her arms like it was her little baby. And the rescue crew told her that they thought it might have kept her from getting washed away, sort of like an anchor.

Next slide. We don't have a whole lot more to go. Here you see—hold on, there's the telephone. (Pause. Change of pitch in tape whine) Sorry, folks, but it was a wrong number. A wrong number. Story of your little girl's life, huh? Just joking. Now. In case you're wondering, the kids are still playing up a storm over at the Bentons. I can see them from where I'm sitting; they're up in a tree house Robby and the old Mister Benton put up. Anyway, here's the place where the road fell out just a few miles down from our house. Looks like a big bear just eased right up to the side of the highway and bit a big chunk out of it. No one was hurt in this slide. Over on Highway One, the Pacific Coast road, the road fell out in two places. Again, nobody hurt. Just lucky this time. Not like the story we heard about the brothers who were walking up the driveway of their house because they heard some noise outside, and the mud came down the driveway from the hill above the house—it *was* the hill above the house—and it rushes down on them with such force that it rips the clothes off one man and carries away the other never to be seen again. (Pause)

So things could be better. But they could be a whole lot worse. Mama, Daddy, I wanted you to hear all this. Oh, wait, the kids are coming back, and I'll bet they'll want to say goodbye. Go on to the last slide, just one more. See us? I know you'll be disappointed, but I wanted to tell you that I have thought long and hard about it . . . and I have decided to stay, natural disasters or otherwise. With my luck, I'm thinking maybe I just belong out here. (Pause) I've got a job beginning next week at a big drugstore in Santa Cruz—they've been busy because of the way people lost a lot of things in the storm up here and need to replace them, and because, I guess, people just keep on struggling during both sickness and in health, storms and sunny days. Mrs. Benton, she's a grandmother herself, she's volunteered to help out with the kids when they're not in school. See her, she's that woman standing with the kids in this last picture? She sort of looks a little like you, doesn't she, Mum? (Pause) Mum, I miss you. And the kids miss you, both of you. Maybe you'll come out and see us. Maybe for Easter? We're going to have the house fixed up real nice again by then. What? Hey, here's the kids again. And I do hope you're feeling better, Daddy. David . . .

(Pause. Whine, rumble of voices gathering behind the hiss of tape)

Bye, Grandpa. Bye Grandmummy.

Muffin?

Bye, Gwandma, bye Gwandpa. (Pause)

It's me again. Last slide. Bye. And wasn't it a good idea, spending that money for the tape machine and camera? We're all set now to send you more slides and tapes. I'll let you know how my new job turns out. And whether—Whoops! There's the telephone! (Faint ringing in distance) David! David, don't you—Bye again, and next time I hope I've got better news to tell you from this side of the (click of cassette, end of reel).

SOURCES OF
COUNTRY MUSIC

Take the Music City tour. That's what Brenda's up and doing, risen up out of that steamy bed where Billy is snoring like something out of a Florida gator farm, showering, dressing in her best jeans and jean jacket—the one with the wagon wheels and cactus embroidered by her Gran—and leaving the room in the Shoney's Motor Inn without, as far as she could tell, Billy stirring more than once.

George Jones is singing on the loudspeaker in the hallway that's leading her toward the lobby. His voice makes Brenda give a shrill little laugh, because it's one of Billy's favorites, and she's smiling to herself, full-mouth, as she walks into the lobby, thinking about how glad she is she's here, and married, and she's only just a little bit nervous about taking the tour by herself. She couldn't feel all that awkward about going alone, not after growing up by herself in Gran's house after her folks died in that crash, not after all the nights she and girlfriends have spent going out to bars (one or two times even as far away together as Birmingham). If she could hear her boot heels clacking on the floor, that would give her confidence, walking like a cowgirl. But there's only carpeting here.

And a rat-nosed old man behind the desk.

"Taking the tour?" he asks, brushing the shoulder of his red blazer as he looks up from his newspaper.

"Good morning. How'd you guess?" Brenda delivers her medium-priced smile.

"It's the time," the man replies, gesturing with a puffy hand toward the thick glass door to the street where the light of a March morning seems pale compared to sunshine down in Selma. "Here she is," he says, his hand still in the air— it's as if he's about to cue in an invisible band—as a dark van with a guitar and Stetson painted on the side and

BLACK JACK TOURS
MUSIC CITY
USA

beneath them pulls up outside the door.

"That's me," Brenda says, still heavy with the thoughts of absent Billy. But in a moment she's out the door, allowing a bearded, pot-bellied fellow in faded blue workshirt and jeans to slide open the side of the van. He nods his silent confirmation. Once she's up into the vehicle, hitching onto the seat next to a woman with weather-worried skin and a man with thinning hair, she can hear the driver calling in a deep pleasant voice through the glass door to the clerk behind the desk, "Have a Nice Day," and she's determined to have a good time.

"Howdy," the woman says with a smile, "we're the Ravens and we're on our way from Florida to Iowa."

"Own a farm," the man says, staring out at the traffic. It's a Saturday, so there doesn't seem to be much of it, and when their bearded guide and driver climbs up behind the wheel and steers them toward the roadway, there's no wait before roaring off on their tour.

"NOW FOLKS," his voice flares up out of a loudspeaker in the roof of the van, "Now Folks," he modulates the voice but it's still loud and metallic though he's sitting only just in the seat in front of them, "I'd like to welcome you to Nashville and say thanks for choosing Black Jack Tours." He clears his throat, and Brenda thinks again of Billy, his eyelids all buttery with fatigue, as he sank down beneath the covers when they came in from their night of celebrating.

"Pretending we're a crowd," says the farm woman, Mrs. Raven.

"His voice reminds me of my husband's," Brenda says.

Mrs. Raven nods. "You lose him? I'm sorry."

"Oh, no, no," Brenda is quick to answer. "We just got in real late and he was too tired to get out of bed."

"We lost a boy," Mrs. Raven says.

"Oh, I'm sorry," Brenda says.

"Ten years ago," Mrs. Raven says, bumping her husband on the shoulder.

"Ten years?" says Mr. Raven, still staring straight ahead.

"Farm machine," Mrs. Raven says.

"I'm sorry," Brenda says. "My own folks got killed in a car accident when I was a little girl myself. I got raised by my Gran, my Mama's mama. My Gran, she's the one embroidered this jacket I'm wearing."

The farm woman scrutinizes the stitching, and then says, "She's awful pretty with her needle."

"Thank you," Brenda says, settling into her place on the seat.

The speaker has been crackling static all this while, but now the driver-guide bursts out again.

". . . WE'VE GOT A STIMULATING three hours for you here, folks, right here in Music City and its environs. . . ."

"I didn't know it was going to be all that long," she says with a sigh. Her picture of Billy hulking there under the covers keeps fading in and fading out, in and out, like the tour guide's voice over that microphone. But darn it, she says to herself, making her fists into little balls of knuckle.

"FOLKS, OUR FIRST STOP in this panoramic visit to our capital of country music, is the birthplace of the Grand Ole Opry and a national landmark, the Ryman Auditorium. . . ."

He double-parks the van, he's out of his seat, out the door, and around the side of the van, sliding open the panel and offering to help Brenda down onto the roadway.

"Thank you," she says, refusing his hand, thinking how quick he is despite that big beer belly. The sun bursts out from behind a layer of cloud and Brenda squints her way into the arched entrance of the large brick building. Inside the low-ceilinged auditorium smells of must and wood. The floors creak. A few other tourists stand at the souvenir booth at the rear of the hall. Brenda and the Ravens pause on the stage, peek into the dressing rooms. Brenda imagines the farm couple with their little boy, sitting in front of the radio out on that Iowa farm, Saturday nights listening to the Opry. The floor gives a good series of creaks for emphasis. She remembers watching TV, TV, TV, with her Gran, the woman embroidering pillows, bedspreads, later her jean jacket, clutching the lapels to ward off a little chill.

"So small," says Mr. Raven as they return to the van, the first remark he's made, really, since the tour began. Brenda's thinking about the hall, small, and then she kicks herself in her mind for not stopping at the souvenir booth.

"NOW FOLKS CAN YOU TELL ME—" They're rolling along now through the middle of the city and it reminds her of the school tour she once took in Birmingham and how everybody kept hoping to see the governor—here's the Tennessee State Capitol right alongside them—him cruising along the sidewalk perhaps in his wheelchair, and Billy was there messing around in the back of the bus with his buddies, the same boys enlisted with him and went to the DMZ. And now he's working, Brenda goes on to herself, as though she's taking inventory in the medical laboratory where she works, he's at the military school, security, and we've got the car almost paid for, and the ladies' man has settled down—we're married.

"—WHAT INDUSTRY is Nashville's largest? What industry, folks?"

Mr. Raven sits suddenly forward and says, "Music!"

"SORRY," the driver blasts out over the speaker, "but as much as we'd like to think it's true, sadly it's not. It's *in*surance, the *in*surance industry, folks, and after *in*surance, believe it or not, the publishing industry. That's right, Nashville, music capital of our United States, is a book town, a print town, with Bibles and sheet music taking the lead over records as the city's most famous product. . . ."

"You live and learn," Mr. Raven says slouching back in his seat.

"Indeed you do," says his wife in reply.

Brenda is studying the traffic, the buildings squat and marble beneath the broad and cloudy sky.

". . . PASSING THE CITY JAIL!" the driver is saying, "WHERE A FAMOUS country singer had a heart attack and died. Can you tell me who that was?"

"We don't know," Brenda says without even giving the Ravens a chance to speak for themselves.

"TEX RITTER," the driver intones, catching Brenda's eye in the rearview mirror. "Tex Ritter died in the Nashville jail house." But this turns out to be a joke, since he goes on to explain that Ritter had arrived at police headquarters to inquire about a nephew who had been arrested because of some delinquent parking tickets and, while there, the singer felt his heart give out. He died.

Brenda's not sure how much time has gone by, but they're picking up momentum now, crossing the bridge over the Cumberland River—she doesn't know this, the Ravens don't, the driver tells them—passing through poor neighborhoods, and pretty soon the houses of people pretty rich. There's Earl Scruggs's house, their guide tells them; there's Earl himself, fetching the Saturday A.M. mail from his postbox. Hey, Earl! Let's all wave! They wave. He's waving back! Earl Scruggs, ladies and gentlemen, the immortal picker himself! And then there's Barbara Mandrell's church, the Willie Nelson and Family Music Store, they're heading northeast toward Old Hickory Lake, he tells them, toward . . .

HELLO DARLIN

It's Twitty City! Conway's enclave, with his famous song, and greeting in raised bricks in the wall along the highway. They don't slow down; they'll come back, the driver explains, and the next thing Brenda knows they're up the road aways, turning right onto a dirt road bumping them along toward the lake.

"THAT TRAILER THERE FOLKS is where the Cash family caretaker lives."

"They got a caretaker," Brenda hears herself saying, her chest filling up with breath to be breathed.

"AND HERE'S the spot where, one night, a car full of members of the Man in Black's family—"

"The Man in Black," the farmer says.

"Oh, I can tell what's coming." Brenda bluffs out all that air.

"—and another car full of fans of his, like yourselves, was passing by . . ."

Mrs. Raven lays a hand on Brenda's arm. "Don't you think about it now, honey. Or if you have to, think it's a song."

"How'd you know I was?"

"*I* was. Why wouldn't *you* be?"

They're talking, feeling deep inside themselves, and when they look up the driver has them turning around in front of the fence that surrounds the house they've come to gawk at, a series of large connected boxlike buildings made of redwood, set down at the edge of the lake.

"It's as big as my whole apartment complex down in Selma," Brenda says.

"That's where you and Granma is living?"

"Me and my husband," Brenda says, staring out beyond the gate.

"Oh, and I forgot that. I'm sorry, darling."

"That's all right," Brenda says. "It's all so new I could forget sometimes myself. Why you know—" They've turned completely around and the redwood house with its guardian fence is drifting behind them. Woods quickly block the view, and they're bumping up that rocky road back to the highway.

"What's that, darling?" The farm woman's voice sounds awfully familiar to Brenda just for that minute—her husband is looking away, away out the window toward the receding woods, the disappearing house and lake.

"Nothing," Brenda says. "Sometimes I don't even know what's on my mind. Here it is, half the tour is almost over, and it seems like no time at all."

"NOW," breaks in their tour guide, "NOW HERE WE ARE," and it seems again but a moment, "ABOUT to make that stop I promised you, at TWITTY CITY, folks, Conway's own little kingdom."

They approach that wall again, and turn into the wide drive just before it, parking in the paved area in front of the high-gated, brick-enclosed compound. A gift shop and small amphitheater stand outside the walls.

"You know what I like," the plain-faced farmer is saying as they step out of the van. "I like the way it's all one big family."

"It is a little like coming to your rich uncle's house," Brenda says to both farmers and to neither. He's got such sad, half-lidded eyes she can't bear to meet them—she's showing something even more painful than him. "Though I never had a rich uncle with a big house like that to come to." She stops on the way to the entrance to the shop and peers through the wide bars of the compound gate. There's a large white building with pillars, like something out of old Selma, and beyond that a row of bright brick condominiums, something like—though twice as solid looking—like the Wind Tree where she and Billy moved in a few days before.

"He built those condos for his children," a voice says in her ear. It's the guide. She doesn't recognize his voice at first, naked as it is without the microphone.

"I hoped I could build one for mine sometime," Brenda says, glancing at him and then back through the gate.

"You've got children?" The guide can't hide his disappointment, an emotion Brenda didn't think she'd produce when she quickly decided to make her own situation clear.

"Not yet, I just got married two days ago," she says, and allows him a warm, though quick, smile.

The guide sighs a sigh like static over his loudspeaker in the van, and says, "Going to come inside? They got a lot of things to choose for souvenirs. You'll want to take something home to your husband."

"I'd planned on it, thank you," Brenda says, twisting around on the boot heel there in front of the gate. "He's back waiting for me at the motel. I know he's going to be so sorry he missed the tour."

"*I* would," the guide says right back to her, his meaning clear and bold.

Brenda normally doesn't get huffy. Normally she wouldn't even blink at a remark like his. But just two days married, two days! And he knows it! You'd think that he would try to curb his behavior. All this she's thinking as she glares at him, and then follows the farm couple as quickly as she can in her boots to the entrance of the store. She's holding a red satin jacket just like Conway's in her hand, fortunately the right size, when there's a commotion on the other side of the racks of cowboy shirts and jackets, by the door near the record albums, and she wanders in that direction. The Ravens have already headed out the door. Brenda drops the jacket on the counter and, with an appeal with upraised hand to the woman at the register, goes outside herself. She sees her tour companions in front of the gate to the compound. Only a few yards on the other side, standing next to a long dark automobile, talking to the driver, is a man of medium height with the thick-browned face of a diesel driver, a Nashville Sounds baseball cap on his head, a satin jacket—telling point—slung over one shoulder, and blue running shoes.

"Conway? It's Conway!" Brenda gives a schoolgirl's little jump up and down in her boots.

"So be it," says Mrs. Raven.

"Conway!" Brenda calls out, pressing close to the bars.

"Conway," the farmer says, quietly, as though in prayer.

The man in the baseball cap and satin jacket turns, breaks into a grin, and waves.

"Hello, darlin'," they hear him say in a gravelly baritone. Then he's climbing into the back seat of the long black car and is gone.

"Conway Twitty, folks," the tour guide says behind them, as though he's still holding his microphone in front of his lips.

Brenda turns, feeling her forehead crinkling, the kind of thing that gives you lines after years and years of frowning.

"Did you *arrange* that?" she asks.

"I'd like to say I have the power," the guide says, "but it's just our lucky day." He smiles at Brenda, showing tobacco-stained teeth. "So what'd you get your husband for a souvenir?"

"Why, I nearly forgot!" Brenda doesn't care about showing alarm in front of him, though so little has passed between them. Boys like this. It's what she married to get away from! "Darn it all!" she says, and runs hip-hip-hop in those boots back into the store. By the time she comes out again, package in hand, the farm couple has climbed back into the van. So has the driver. They're waiting for her, the engine running. She climbs in. The vehicle pulls out of the parking lot and heads back toward the highway, back toward town, and she's sitting quietly, remembering Conway—his voice, his face. He seems more real to her, even in memory, than her recollection of the sleeping Billy back at the motel, and she doesn't like that.

"IT'S NEARLY THAT TIME, FOLKS," the driver says in their ears, and Brenda doesn't even flinch at the noise level, though as with electric music she knows her ears will be ringing later on. "ONE MORE STOP ON THE TOUR, on this particular route, because we do have others, Nashville by Night, Opryland, which includes an evening at the Opry itself. . . ."

"We've got tickets for tonight," Brenda says to the farm wife.

"Why so do we," the woman responds. "Don't we, Mel?"

The farmer has been staring out the window—familiar sights, now that they're heading back the way they've come, the Willie Nelson and Family store, the subdivision where they saw the greatest living picker of them all, the bridge over the Cumberland. There must be other sights to see but this is the route they have taken.

"Do we?" he says.

"Which show?" Brenda is feeling something, thinking.

"First," the woman says.

"Oh," Brenda says. "We got the second. Billy likes the late show, usually. But maybe we could arrange to meet in-between. Be nice if you could meet Billy."

"That'd be real nice," the farm wife says, "if we can arrange it. Don't you say so, Mel?"

That farmer—he appears to be lost in the sights again, and his wife has to jiggle his shoulder to get him to respond.

"Thinking about spring planting, are you?" his wife teases.

"Thinking about our boy," he replies.

"THE FINAL STOP on our little tour this morning, folks, the Country Music Hall of Fame and Museum . . ." the guide, doing his job, breaks in.

"That's right by our motel!" Brenda says, glad to have something to say.

"You're a lucky girl," the farm wife says. "The two of you."

"I know," Brenda says, reading into the woman's words everything that's there. "Really."

Now here's the museum, just across the road from their motel—a great location. It's warmer in the parking lot here than out at Twitty City. Spring is coming on even this far north, and she feels warm *in*side after they pay their admission and pass into the exhibition—because there's Elvis's own white Eldorado, and when Mrs. Raven comes up next to her and pushes the button on the little fence between them and the car and roof goes back and they can see the gold records inlaid in the ceiling, and the bar and the TV, too, she hears the woman take in a deep breath.

"Father," says the farm wife, "it would have been worth coming all the way *just* for this."

"I suppose," the farmer says, reminding Brenda of her own tight-lipped Billy.

She edges along to the next exhibit, and, standing there in front of the place on the wall where they put Patsy Cline's own cigarette lighter, the one they found at the site where she died in that airplane crash, Brenda can sense real heat coming on, inside and out, and she strips off her jacket, folding it over her arm. That crash! the flames! the fiery end! She gives a shiver—how can you feel so cold thinking about things so hot?—and moves along to watch some videos of the old-time performers, stopping in time to tap her toes, rock back and forth on her heels to some old-timer she never heard of singing "The Orange Blossom Special." She smiles at his yodeling, then slows down to listen to the Carter Family wail slow and deep and broad-noted, "Amazing Grace." She looks around for the farm couple, wants to say, "That's the in-laws of the Man in Black." She knows that much. But they're nowhere in sight. So she keeps on moving. Now she steps into a room full of photographs of the living greats: Crystal, with her long rug of hair flying up and all around her, the picture catching her in mid-leap toward some high note Brenda can imagine clearly in her mind—Crystal, now there's a nice sounding name for a little baby girl—and there's Kenny, white-haired, bearded, distinguished at an early age, and Merle, a face of experience, eyes full of confidence. It's all like a family album, and she wants to say that to the farm couple, but they're still nowhere in sight. She wants to say how she knows these people, though she doesn't know them, all these real, familiar faces.

But as she's looking around, what catches her eye from across the room but the powerful shapes and colors of a painting. Clacking her way across the parquet floor, she gets close enough to read the plaque alongside the canvas. "Sources of Country Music," the sign tells her, a painting commissioned by Tex Ritter from his friend, artist Thomas Hart Benton.

It's the finest work of art Brenda's ever seen! The banjo picker on the side, the women with their unfurled skirts before them, the steamboat churning down the river, the railroad train racing on the shore, its dark smoke steaming behind it like a flag—and on the right-hand side the cowboy twanging his guitar, the fiddlers, more women dancing, clap your hands and stomp your feet, the land coming up in spring.

"Billy?"

No answer from the other side of the motel room door, no sound of TV, nothing. She spins around, clutching the package to her chest, to see the Mustang parked just where they had left it last night. On the other side of the parking lot lies the restaurant, and she starts walking toward it. Once she arrives she feels unsure, looks around smelling the meat, eggs, the lightest touch of grease, coffee in the air, cigarettes, all with the chatter of the lunch crowd in the background. Everyone here looks like the Ravens. But none of them's them.

"How y'all today?" the hostess greets her. "One?"

Brenda gives her only the smallest glimpse of her usually friendly smile and says, "I'm looking for my . . ."

What stops her? She sees a tall waitress with her back to her, her left hand crossed over her waist and cupping her right elbow while her right hand is placed flat against the right side of her face. She's got long braids, and one dangles loosely to the right of her neck, the other straight down. Brenda can't see her eyes, but her posture says that she might be smiling. A cloud of smoke billows up around her, and Brenda pushes forward through the room.

"Gol," Billy says, looking up at her, "I woke up so hungry I coulda ate a car. Hey, you have a good tour? Sit you down here and tell me about it." The waitress slides away as if on greased shoes.

"It was real nice," Brenda says, following the other woman's departure toward the salad bar, "but I want you to come up and see something now."

"See what?"

"I just want you to come across the street and see something."

Billy narrows his dark puffy eyes and picks up his cigarette, cowboylike is how Brenda thinks of it, cowboylike and almost mean. There's a flicker in his eyes , too, that she can't explain and doesn't want to try, except that she sparks another look herself off in that same direction, and she catches a glimpse of that waitress holding still like some forest animal at the edge of a clearing before dashing off to the other end of the room.

"I want you to see something, Billy," she repeats herself.

"Car?" he says. "Some car I'd like?"

"You could see a car, that's part of it. But not the whole thing."

"Well, I'll come look at a car," he says, reluctantly rising from his chair. He makes a big show about leaving a tip, something unusual for him, and there's something new about his mouth, too, something that she can't describe, or maybe it's just something she never noticed before.

"Now what is it, honey?"

They're walking across the parking lot, boots clacking together. Brenda's still holding her package; Billy's lighted another cigarette.

"Something in the Country Music Museum," she says, looking up. "I was just there on the tour." The clouds have parted—a long trail of birds returning north gives her something to concentrate on.

"What y'all see?" he asks, taking her elbow and squeezing, coming back to her, as if out of deep sleep.

"Lots of things," she says. "It was real interesting. I met some real nice people, and we saw Johnny Cash's house—and Billy, we met Conway. Oh," she says, hugging her package, "here—here I was carrying this. But I was looking for you." She hands it over.

He stops in the middle of the roadway and takes the jacket out of the paper sack.

"Well," he says. "Well, well. Well. Well. Thanks. Well, here," he says, handing it back. "You carry it now, hey?"

Brenda shivers again, a little chill around her heart part of the chest, but she takes it from him, stuffing it back into the sack.

"Now here?" he says, stepping up to the entrance of the museum. It's clear from the way he's working his head that he hasn't counted on going into a building like this as part of his morning.

"We got to pay," Brenda says. "But I got it." And she takes some money from her little leather bag and hands it over to the woman sitting in the booth in the middle of the entrance hall.

"They got Elvis's car here?" Billy says, looking up at a sign.

"They got all that," Brenda says. "They got Patsy Cline's cigarette lighter, you know, the one they found where her plane crashed? And lots of things, but I want you to see something first."

She takes him by the hand and leads him to the room with the photographs and the painting. Now look at this, she says to him with her eyes. And guides him forward to the wall, maybe four feet back from it.

"Uh-huh," he says.

"Now look at it," she says.

"I'm looking." He looks over at her.

"Well?" she says.

"Well what?" he says, looking back at her.

"Well, doesn't that just get you?" she says.

"That picture? Not me," Billy says. "It'll take a lot more than that to get me."

FISHING FOR COYOTES

In a South Texas bus station on Christmas Eve day, a delicate-appearing young woman with a ruddy face and sandy hair, an infant in her arms, steps down from a dust-streaked Greyhound. Next out of the bus is her husband, a tall man slightly older in appearance, with a shock of thick black hair. He carries a suitcase and wears several shoulder bags bulging with clothing.

"You know you can do your sketch when we get to their house," the woman says. "Uncle Ben is probably waiting for us." She leads the man into the waiting room, looks around, and heads out through the street door, hugging the baby close to her chest, even though Corpus Christi feels only a few degrees colder than the town to the south where they boarded the bus the night before. Having spent her childhood here, she knows that at Christmas a storm can blow up out of nowhere, and so she has come prepared.

"If it's OK with you, I think I'll sit down and try to start it until he gets here," her husband says.

The woman—her name is April—searches the roadway that runs along the beach, leading down to the bay.

"I see him!" she says, the relief showing in her voice. "It *is* him. Uncle Ben! Hi! We're here!" she calls out, although there is no chance that the man behind the wheel of the large blue car can hear her. But he sees her and waves back. She glances at her husband and down at the sleeping child. She doesn't want two infants on her hands—not with all of their luggage and a Christmas holiday with her mother to deal with. When her uncle, a huge man who has to work himself slowly out from behind the wheel of the car, waddles up to them, she rushes forward with the baby and throws herself into his arms.

"Your mama's going to do a cartwheel when she sees this little thing, honey," Ben says, and his voice booms in the parking lot. "We all been looking forward to meeting you, William." He thrusts a beefy hand past April's shoulder and shakes her husband's fist. "Hear you're an artist."

"That's right," William says, "but you can't tell too easily, because I shaved my beard."

April steps back from the two men, enjoying the presence of this uncle who is a bloated version of the father she remembers, a newspaperman who wrote for the East Texas daily where Ben still runs the pressroom.

William narrates the saga of his Mexican haircut and shave while they load their belongings into the trunk of Ben's car. A few spins of the wheel and they are rolling along past the harbor, where a row of new motels mars April's vision of the beach of her childhood. Small, fast-moving clouds with bright fringes and dark undersides mark the horizon where the bay meets the gulf. The weather is just as she remembers it—a mixture of promise and menace.

By the time they arrive at the small brick ranch-style house on the outskirts of town, William seems to have forgotten that he was angry that she wouldn't let him sit down right away and sketch the sunrise he had seen from the bus as they crossed the border into Texas. He assists April with the baby while Ben attacks the luggage. But no one can help April with the fear that arises when she enters the house.

In the narrow foyer, she catches the scent of her mother's whiskey breath and chokes at the smell. But when her mother appears in front of her, suddenly old, her hair gone all silver, the choking becomes a sob. April opens her arms to her mother and clasps her around the shoulders the way she has seen prize fighters do on television.

Ben ambles up alongside of them, holding the baby. "Where do I put this package, lady?"

April's mother frees herself from her daughter and snatches up the child as though saving it from a fire. "I d-don't even remember her name!" she says with a wail.

"Marina, Mama. It's from Shakespeare. Don't scare her now with your crying."

Aunt Sal, Ben's wife, dark-complected, her hair heaped up on her head like a pile of leaves, comes over to greet April with a whiskey kiss.

"And here's the man responsible," Ben says, nudging William toward Sal.

Husband and aunt shake hands, unable to find much to say to each other. They glance at the child, who is now alert, dribbling sounds down her chin.

"You must be real tired from sitting up all night on the bus," says Sal, who has been April's mother's landlady ever since she sold her small rancher and moved to town.

"I hope we're not going to be too much trouble," April says.

"No trouble at all," says Sal, taking her first full look at William, who is interpreting for April's mother the noises coming from Marina. "Just you and your mama keep out of each other's hair and we'll have us a big old Christmas."

"You're getting along OK?" April asks, her voice a whisper.

"I enjoy keeping your mama, and she enjoys being kept."

And it is true that in the next hours there seems to be little friction between the women.

"It's only between me and Mother that the sparks fly," April says to William later, in the afternoon, when they have been relieved of baby duty and installed, for a "nappie," as Sal calls it, in a bedroom far to the rear of the house.

"How about some friction between us?" William says in the tone he must have used on all of the women he brought up to the loft before their marriage, a tone she once found irresistible.

"This won't help at all," April says, batting aside his groping hands. But they lie beneath the covers, and only faint sounds of laughter reach them through the thick door. What happens next seems to her as inevitable as the romance that followed their meeting on a Seventh Avenue downtown local, the marriage that followed the romance, and the baby that followed before the year was out.

They awake into Christmas Eve. Ben has invited April to come outside while he lights the luminarias—stubby white candles stuck into sand at the bottom of paper sacks. It is a custom that she had forgotten. But, standing at her uncle's side, she recalls how, when she was a child she enjoyed this little ceremony and how, later, just after she entered high school, when her father was already ill and her mother drinking steadily, she and some friends walked past house after house, kicking over the neat rows of glowing orange sacks.

"Tell me about that newspaper job," Ben says, tamping down the sand in those sacks unprotected from the breeze by the hedge or the line of shrubs.

"How did you hear about that?"

"You listed me as a reference. They called me."

April frowns, still a little surprised that the newspaper people would care that much about her application. At college in the north, she had never paid much attention to the campus paper, let alone written for it. But after graduation, when she realized that she was either going to have to find work or return home, it occurred to her that she ought to apply for a job in New York City. At the time, what had drawn her to her father's profession was its loose hours and the prospect of seeing her name in print. Now she remembered a saying of his, one that she had repeated to herself over and over again during the subway ride up to the office of the *Times* on that lonely first day in New York—"Every story worth its bacon opens with a hook."

The wind shifts and April kneels, using her body to shelter a sack as she lights the candle inside it. "They eventually offered me a job as a copygirl, Uncle Ben, but I had to turn it down. I was pretty far along with Marina by then. Anyway, we had already found out about the school in Mexico where I'm teaching. We decided it would be the best thing for both of us if I do this kind of work for now—while William paints."

Uncle Ben cups his meaty fist around a cigarette and lights it with the same ease with which he ignites the candles in the sacks. He puffs on the cigarette and the wind scatters sparks across the lawn. "You like teaching those diplomatic brats?"

"Nothing I want to do for the rest of my life. But for now it's OK, Uncle Ben."

"Have time to enjoy your baby down there?"

"We have a sort of maid-babysitter. She comes in while I go to school." Anticipating his next question, she adds, "William works in his studio at home."

"He sells things?"

"He's just getting started, Uncle Ben. He's got a little money that comes in from an aunt who died last year."

"Nice going. When your Aunt Sal passes, she'll leave you the recipe for her barbecue sauce."

"He's not rich at all," she assures him.

"No," Ben says, "not if you come on the bus. Was it a good ride? I ain't been down that way for years."

April thinks back to the dark desert road, the baby and William asleep while she stared out into the blackness in fear of her meeting with her mother. "It was OK."

"But nothing you want to do for the rest of your life."

They laugh, then move along to light the remaining candles. When they are finished, Ben hugs April and she feels his barrel chest against her, big as the whole state of Texas.

Inside the house, the drinking has already begun.

"What a nice young man this is!" Aunt Sal declares. "I'm so sorry he shaved his beard! I wanted to see how a real artist looks!"

"I told Sal we didn't want to have any hassles at the border," William says.

April catches a glimpse of her mother pouring herself another Scotch. Then, before she knows it, she has had three herself, and she stops thinking about anything except sweet little Marina, who sleeps peacefully in the rented crib in a room down the hall from their own. William, under the direction of Sal, now gathers together the pails he and Ben will need when they drive over to the Mexican side of town to pick up the tamales for the Christmas Eve supper. She is pleased that William is having such a good time—she knows he must be, since he's made no further mention of his sunrise sketch.

She doesn't feel abandoned, the way she often does when William leaves her with the baby. Her mother and aunt appear much more benign than she remembers. If Marina wakes up, they will help her, she feels sure. It's a miracle that the baby doesn't wake, their voices ring so sharply through the room. They're talking about old times—many buckets of tamales ago, as Aunt Sal puts it. April's mother doesn't protest. She takes a sip of her Scotch and sags forward, as though someone had let the air out of her, head on chest. In a moment, she is snoring.

"She just loves being a grandmother so much," Sal says. "She made a promise to herself—no more quarreling with you."

"She'll just pass out, instead."

Sal purses her lips and touches them to the rim of her glass. "I guess nothing much happened to you up north except you got yourself a husband and a baby."

April stares at her aunt until the woman finally lowers her eyes and sips her drink. "How's Arvin? Still selling Coke?"

"Your cousin is doing just fine. He opened one of those drive-in food restaurants up in Lubbock, and he's making himself a nice living. He's working tomorrow—only place in town open on Christmas. Figure he'll make a week's money in one day."

"That's nice," April says, trying to keep scorn for her big-eared cousin from showing in her voice.

After a long silence, her aunt asks, "How come you turned down that good job?"

April sits up nervously, glancing over at her slumbering mother. "Did she ask you to find out for her after she passed out?"

"Aw, honey, I was just wondering. They called your Uncle Ben, you know."

"He told me," April says.

She excuses herself and attempts to walk a straight line for the bathroom down the hall, but bounces off one wall and then the other. "Like mother like daughter," she tells herself with the same scorn that crept into the question about her cousin. Before she knows it, she has turned on the bathroom faucet. She undoes her slacks and gushes into the bowl. She could be five years old again. But when she is ready to return to her aunt, a look in the mirror on the medicine chest reassures her that she's herself, ruddy-cheeked, sandy-haired, green-eyed. She flicks her tongue across her lips as though she were about to step into a room full of New York partygoers where she might meet the man of her life. Then, as she joins Sal in the living room, she hears her father laugh.

It is Ben laughing. He and William have returned with the tamales.

The rest of the evening slurs by. With her knees pressed against the edge of a plastic TV tray, April takes her first bite of the traditional midnight supper and tells William that she feels like Proust's Marcel.

"Who?" he asks drunkenly. Then he says, "Oh, yeah."

Outside the window, paper sacks go up in flames as the wind shifts off the bay. April's mother sits up long enough to bid everyone Merry Christmas and to all a good night. Ben and Sal soon excuse themselves, leaving April with a William suddenly morose.

"The sketch," she says.

"You can read my mind."

Then he slinks off to bed and she's listening to the house quiet down. Suddenly she leaps to her feet and rushes down the hall. Sure enough, Marina has awakened. April changes her in the crib, picks her up, and, pacing the room, rocks her back to sleep. She attempts to exhale her whiskey breath away from the baby's face, but it is hopeless. How many nights did her own mother spray her with the sweet metallic whiskey droplets of her breath? She paces and rocks, singing to her baby, saying to herself Merry Christmas and to all a good night.

"Merry Christmas!" April's mother, baby in arms, surprises them in bed. Shaking off sleep, April peers through blurred eyes at her mother's bright face.

"What time it is?" Her voice sounds crackly and parched, the way her mother's voice ought to sound but doesn't.

"Later than you think! Arvin called early, woke everybody up. I've been to church already."

"Jesus!" William says from beneath the covers.

"Blasphemer!" April's mother calls to him, half serious.

"Who took care of Marina while you—"

"Ben and Sal. Come on up, you-all. We're heading out for the picnic."

April collects herself. Her mother has made such a remarkable recovery, she thinks there might be hope for her. She nudges William, who reeks of last night's fiesta. He burrows deeper into the covers. In the shower, she raises her arms as if surrendering to a lawman and lets hot water pound away at her back.

"Where's this picnic again?" William asks as they trundle out to the car—the two of them, April's mother with baby in arms, Ben and Sal carrying baskets of food.

"On Padre Island," April replies, trying to make sense of the feeling of great warmth that overwhelms her at the sight of her mother holding little Marina. The woman hasn't had a drink yet and it's two hours since breakfast. Sal bumps hips with April when William holds open the rear door of the car, and motions for her to slide onto the seat.

"I'm sitting next to this gal," she says, "'cause I still got some unanswered questions."

April sits behind Ben, who drives the large Buick as though it were a motorboat, swaying from one side of the road to the other, following mysterious patterns of waves on the highway leading south. William looks through the window at the flat land stretching out in all directions. In the front passenger seat grandmother and baby make noises at one another.

Sal asks April how she and William met.

"On the Seventh Avenue downtown local just after I'd come back from applying for that job at the *New York Times*," April says.

Sal asks her about their wedding, a ceremony they wrote themselves in William's downtown loft. "Everything's downtown in New York City. At least, that's how it seems to me,"

Sal says. "You know how unhappy we all were that we couldn't come up for it, but Ben had to work, and your mama, she just wasn't feeling well at the time. And then along came that beautiful little critter, that Marina! We sure wished we were up there to see when she arrived!"

"Maybe we can all stay in better touch from now on," April says. "Life up north gets kind of . . . disconnected from family things."

"Hey!" says Ben from behind the wheel. "How come you let them Yankees beat your accent out of you!"

"I like her accent," William says, his first words of the entire ride. "I want her to keep it."

"He shinks it's cute," Aunt Sal says, slurring her words as though she'd had a few drinks. But April can smell her breath—it's pure coffee and cigarettes and eggs and bacon.

"This is cute," says April's mother from the front seat, holding aloft a smiling Marina.

Padre Island 3. April shivers at the sign. She begins to explain the family tradition to William, but Sal takes over and it's just the way it was when April was a little girl. "Buster—that's Ben's brother, April's daddy—they used to come out here every Christmas morning with their daddy; he came all the way from Tennessee when he was a boy; now, he was a newspaperman himself. . . ."

The car swings into a left turn onto the causeway connecting mainland to island, and they sway from side to side like passengers on the deck of one of the small steamers April can see on the horizon of the looming slate-grey gulf. She thinks of the poor sailors, of how they must feel to be on the sea instead of in port at a time like this, when any port would pass for home. The thin strip of sand dunes stretches out before them north and south, "like the bent bow of a giant Indian hunter up to his waist in the middle of the gulf aiming a huge arrow at El Paso, far to the west," she once wrote in a school essay, a piece of writing her father found so pleasing that he quoted from it in his column.

"There'll be some nice places where you can sketch," she says over Aunt Sal's lap to William.

"Um," he replies, lost apparently in the vista of low dark-bottomed clouds that lead the way, like stepping stones across a creek, toward the Mexican border.

There's a sudden shift in the car's swaying motion, and the wheels whir in the sand. As Ben turns right and rolls them a short distance down the beach, April wonders idly what it would be like to head directly into the knee-high breakers so that the car was stuck in the sand while the tide rolled in. Marina's cry yanks her from this vision.

"Please cover her head, Mama," she says as they prepare to disembark.

"I think I remember how to take care of a little one on this beach," her mother replies, an edge to her voice which April hasn't heard for years.

"Please," April says, concerned when she opens the door and feels the full blast of the sea wind on her face.

"Come help us," Sal breaks in, alert to the danger of a quarrel. "We got to set this up real quick and get a fire started. William?"

"He wants to do some sketching," April says. "Anyway, I'll do his share over here. You go on, Will."

She sees how her husband admires the seabirds hanging motionless above the breakers. The cries of the gulls blow in with the stiff breeze that keeps them suspended, their beaks pointed toward the turquoise sky to the east, a thin strip of light where the cloud cover falls short of the horizon.

"Sunny in Florida," Ben says, unloading chairs and kettles and bottles and boxes from the trunk of the car as though rescuing heirlooms from a fire. April, unfolding beach chairs, figures that she might as well be niece to a marlin as to this huge man. His life, his motives remain a mystery to her. She can tell by his grin that he's drunk already. What if he didn't bear any resemblance at all to her father, she thinks—would she love him as much then? She brushes her hair out of her eyes, turns to see that William has wandered off southward along the dunes.

"Sunny in Mexico, too," she says.

Her uncle looks up from pulling out the last box from the trunk and motions for Sal, who has been waiting at the open rear door of the car.

"How's it living down there with the Messkins?" he asks April.

"Just like living up north with the snow diggers. I try to be myself and get along with everybody. It's a nice life for the baby so long as we can keep her healthy."

Sal brushes past April and joins Ben over the small platform he has erected in the sand. A yellow-tipped flame leaps unexpectedly above the rim.

"Magic," says April.

"Sterno," says Ben. "Don't you remember?"

"Sure do," April says, and she glances toward the front of the car, where she thinks she hears the baby. But it is a gull shrieking into the wind out where the breakers begin.

"Don't look now, honey," Sal says, touching her arm. "Your southern's coming back. Hey, where's that artist husband of yours? Isn't he going to want some steak?"

"May be against his religion," Ben says. "I hear tell artists are supposed to starve." He slaps himself on his imposing stomach. "Guess I'll just be a laborer all this life. Your daddy, now, there was an artist who could be a laboring man at the same time."

April peers up into the wind, as hungry for news about her father as she is for the steak now sizzling on the makeshift grill.

"Was he, Uncle Ben?" She hears it in her voice, and she is sure Ben hears it, too.

"Come round these parts more often and I'll tell you plenty, April."

April smiles politely. There's a feeling she has, a question she wants to ask, but something catches her eye down the beach, a dark flicker above the water too low to be a leaping fish, too high to be a skimming bird hunting for its holiday brunch. Whatever it is, it's gone.

Ben is speaking, but his words whip away like ashes from the tip of his smoldering cigarette.

Abruptly, April turns to look behind her. Nothing there but the gulf. She's trembling now.

Ben has stopped talking. Excusing herself, April walks over to the car. There, in the front seat, she spies grandmother and granddaughter sleeping. Satisfied with the sight, she walks south along the strand.

Without footprints to guide her—they have either been washed away by the waves or blown away by the warm, stiff breeze—April tracks William by instinct, trying to gauge which particular configuration of light, cloud, sea, sand, and grass, bird in flight, or driftwood might appeal to his eye. There's a certain laxity to his vision she recognizes from having posed for him when they first met. He likes to look at things that appear to have been flung down in front of him, attempting in his drawings to catch the world on the edge of motion. That's how he likes me, with my life in disarray, April thinks. But she can't know for sure. William has never found the words to express what he sees. He talks very little. In that respect, he is just the opposite of her father. And yet the hold he has on her reminds April all too much of the dead newsman who used to lead her along this same beach. It's not just words that can catch you. There are other ways. Mute infants. And dumb shows of love. She has another thought as she's walking, and it startles her. If her father were alive, they'd probably quarrel all the time.

"William?"

As though a hand had flicked the edge of a scarf in her face, the wind slaps her words back at her.

"Will?"

She looks down the beach toward the car, the family now no more than a dark blur on the dunes. To her left are the leaping waters of the gulf, ahead of her the sunny sky above Mexico. At her right, the dunes rise to the height of her chest. She climbs high enough to survey the leeward side of the island.

Here three men stand in a trough between the waves of sand, two of them poised with rods in their hands, their lines stretching beyond the range of dunes that edge the shore. The third man is William, hands at his sides, staring into the grass.

At first, she thinks the two men have gone mad, casting into the sand rather than into the ocean at their backs. Then she recalls the old custom of baiting hooks with savory bits of meat to attract coyotes, those wild scavengers with a bounty on their heads who made the dunes their home. Once, as a child, she had disobeyed her father and wandered away from the Christmas Day picnic, just as William has now, and watched as a lone angler hauled in a yipping, whimpering, patchy-coated coyote, hooked through the jowl.

She doesn't wait to see it happen again. Poor William, she thinks, as she stumbles her way back among the dunes, recalling his empty hands: he had no intention of sketching anything. In her struggle this morning with her family, she hadn't even noticed that he never brought his materials along with him. A high-pitched shriek, but whether of beast or bird or woman or baby she cannot immediately determine, rises suddenly on the wind. Something catches in her throat, and she races along the shifting sand to answer a cry of distress.

THE PAC-MAN MURDERS

Lt was sultry late summer twilight in Oak Ridge when this all began, with a trace of honeysuckle still in the air and me with a lagoon in my dreams. Arlene had gone off to her "drama" group, as she called those evenings, and the kids had just come in from mowing the lawn. I allowed them to drag me off to a new video arcade in Knoxville to show them how easy the games were to figure.

They were skeptical at first—even Super-Dad, as they often referred to me, as much in love, I hoped, as in jest, wouldn't be able to beat these new machines because they were supposed to produce random patterns to ward off geniuses and the like.

"Nothing is random," I remember saying to Junie, and her mouth pursed up in that smile of hers, as though she were deciding right then and there, like some antique eastern goddess of creation, whether to make the universe wholly sweet or wholly tart.

"Nothing, Daddy? Nothing at all?"

We had already gotten underway, I in the front seat of the wagon, Junie in the front passenger seat, and sulky David sitting behind me so that, as it seemed always to have been the case since he was old enough to do more than soil his diapers, he could cause me distress by his presence just at the edge of things. "Name me something that is," I said, working my pipe over to the right side of my jaw. I always try to keep a level tone about me since I'm not sure how smart these kids are, and I remember how it was growing up in a world where nobody had any faith about right answers, unless they sounded right.

"Melting ice cream," David spoke up from the rear, his voice alight with the combatitiveness that so inspired him these days. The sky, too, was on fire, a purplish glow, as though some new volcano in the Pacific archipelago had shot its infernal combustion into the upper atmosphere the week before while we had our heads turned—what were we doing? fishing in the French Broad River? taking in a forties comedy at the Tennessee Theater on Gay Street, the sad main drag of Knoxville with the cheerful name?

"Good try, son. But there's pattern involved in that. Think about the density of the ice cream and the way in which temperature would affect it, and there's always the shape of the scoop itself—allow for a certain amount of wildness within the range, but there's still the range."

"I don't think so," David said, and though I couldn't see his face, I guessed that he was staring back at the violent western sky, not keeping his eyes, as Junie and I were, on the deepening night to the east.

"Take your mother," I tried to counter him. "Now you and your sister know that over the years—"

"Leave her out of this, please," David said, with a tone that made me bite down in my pipe.

"I know something that's completely random," Junie spoke up.

"What's that, Bug?" I asked, steering us down the road like a small boat through smooth ocean. Daylight had all but completely faded, and as we left the limits of our little model city for the highway ahead, I wondered if I could truly predict what was going to happen next—the countryside in these parts has that effect sometimes, of producing pathos beyond the limit, or is it all countryside that does such things?

"Random *House*!" she announced, "that's what!"

"Good try. Because they're random-brained enough, that's right, if they want to publish my stuff."

"False modesty will get you nowhere," Junie said, echoing something she must have heard pass between me and Arlene at the dinner table.

"Well," I was straining to see the hills covered with kudzu vine on either side of us, "the reason I wrote those mystery novels was to give myself the *illusion* that there was something random in the universe. To free myself from the lab. It's a hard life, you know."

"Sure," David said.

"It's true." I insisted, "When I was your age, David, I was already working out in New Mexico."

"Call that work?" He was gathering himself up into a real huff, an imitation, I feared, of one of his mother's moods, and that disturbed me more than his attitude itself—for the behavior patterns in our family to cross gender lines, for Junie to act with my temperament and David to model himself on his mother. It was, I was thinking (still think), a dangerous way to grow.

"Sitting in a room pushing numbers around," he said. "I work harder on my paper route."

"Could be, David. I wouldn't know, though. I never had one."

"It would have taught you something about real life."

"David," Junie said in an agitated voice, "you'd better show some respect."

"Junie, he's perfectly right."

"Nothing's perfectly right," David said.

"And you're perfectly right about that," I said.

"Ha, ha," he laughed as hollowly as the human voice will allow. And then he settled back into silence even as Junie kept up some variations on the theme.

"It seems perfectly right to me that you write mysteries to take your mind off your work, Dad. I just wish you did it under your own name."

"I use a different part of my brain to write them, sweetheart," I told her, "and so I thought that I ought to use another name. Besides, when I first started writing them I wanted to keep it a secret. I didn't know if I could do it, and, well, you know how we are; I just thought it was natural to keep it a secret."

"I hate secrets," Junie said. "I'm tired of secrets."

"We all have them."

"I don't keep them," she said. "I'm opposed to them."

"Sugar," I said, using the local intonation, "you don't need to keep anything you know secret. But sometimes I talk to your mother, and she has to keep secrets."

"Ha!" David sat up in the rear. "I knew it."

"Knew what?" I asked, trying to find his face in the rear-view mirror.

"Mom has secrets."

"Of course she does," I said. "Every woman does."

"Every person," Junie said.

"Every man, woman, child, and . . . opossum," I said.

"Ha, ha!" he said.

By this time we'd rolled along Pellissippi Parkway to the connection with Interstate 40 and headed east to the turn-off for Downtown West—these names and directions are confusing to anyone who doesn't know, and there's hardly a way to make them more exact than they are. But as I often did when this trouble began, I found that the only way to clear my head was to concentrate on a problem, whether it was a plot for a mystery or a plan for an experiment. This sultry evening, when the air at crepuscule turned inky-dark, I did both.

"Super-Dad!" Junie cheered me on, and within ten minutes of our arrival at the video parlor I had attracted a crowd of about a dozen well-laundered and vacant-eyed teenagers as I passed beyond fifty thousand points on one of the Pac-Man machines.

"Super-Dad!" The kids took up the chant when I passed the seventy-thousand mark. At eighty thousand I looked up to find that David was gone.

"Where'd he disappear to?" I asked Junie, stepping away from the bluish-green aura of the game screen. I could hear the whiny cheers and exultation of the kids behind me, but that mattered very little with David not among them.

"Don't follow him," she said. "He'll come back."

"I'm going to take a walk," I said.

She shrugged, held out her hand. I gave her some cash to change into tokens for the other games—she couldn't have wanted to play Pac-Man ever again in the wake of what I'd done—Donkey Kong, Asteroids, Star Shooter, Mr. Whizzer, Galaxies, Harm the Armor, Getaway, Clash; and then I stepped out onto the mall, my shirt dripping sweat. Aside from the pizza place, most of the shops seemed closed. But as I wandered along in an easterly direction, I noticed the inviting lights in the window of the combination bookstore and health food emporium nearly all the way at the end. Dreaming fool that I was, I pictured David hovering above the mystery rack, one of my paperbacks in his hand. A curly-haired, round-faced blonde with eyes that appeared slightly oriental sat behind the cash register squeezing together one of those doodads they sell in such stores in order to keep their heads above water, a monkey connected by his hands to two wooden staves which when squeezed caused him to twirl over and over like a gymnast. On the new book-shelf, I found my latest original, *The Molecule Killer* by Hy Zenburg. "Zenburg," I read from the jacket flap, "is the pseudonym of a well-known American scientist." At the mystery rack, I found three early novels, each in no less than a tenth printing, these stories I'd plotted to keep myself sane in New Mexico and Oak Ridge.

"Can I help you, sir?" the girl asked from behind the register. She had set down her monkey toy and I could see just how bored and beautiful she was.

"Looking for my son," I said. "So, no thanks."

Pieces of a new plot fell into place as I left the store and wandered back along the mall. *The Pac-Man Murders*. Through the window of the arcade I could see Junie hunched over the glowing board of one of the computer games. A tall, thin boy, his face overpowered by a smirk, raised a hand to hail me.

"David," I said, in recognition and farewell, and turned and walked quickly to the car.

As I drove away toward the west, the plot thickened.

There was a scene in a lab, there was a scene in a video parlor, there was a scene at the drama group where wives of physicists congregated, there was a seemingly innocent victim involved in a plutonium smuggling ring, there were

Palestinians, vagrant wives, druggy children. And Hy Zenburg's stalwart physicist hero, Pall Watson, on the job again, working by indirection, his heart wide open to the randomness of things, his intellect urging him to find the pattern, find the key. I wasn't sure, of course, how it all fit together—could it be a case of murder by plutonium poisoning, or merely madness caused by the proximity to such deadly materials? The title led me along and I felt on the verge of piercing the first veil when it happened: a flash of light, a screech of brakes, my own foot slamming on the pedal. I'd broken one of my hard and fast rules—never lose your concentration in southern traffic—and now I was going to pay. My leg ached as I climbed from the car, my wrist swollen, and my throat throbbing rawly with thirst. A bear-size man in Stetson and boots came stumbling around the corner of the sign on the shoulder:

PUSSY CAT VILLAGE

"How you-all tonight?" he said with a mountain twang, and then sidestepped into a ditch. I heard him retching in the dark as I took the path along which he'd come, walking directly past dozens of cars parked neatly in the gravel lot to where another sign said "entrance." Harsh music, cigarette smoke, beer smell, and cheers greeted me when I pushed open the door. Three lanky fellows, these sporting truckers' caps and beards, surged past me out the door, and in the obscure dome of illuminated shadow that hovered over the room, a view as if into the heart of a cloud chamber, I could see crowded table upon table of men with and without hats and caps and hair, and many, many bearded faces, and many faces shaven.

"Five-dollar cover, sir." A man as large as any I'd ever seen in person stepped between me and my view of the central stage which, just that second, had been splashed with the beam of a red-tinted spotlight. "Get it up or get on out!"

"Oh, Lordy," someone moaned as I made my way between tables. I had been staring across the room where a pale-skinned woman with a familiar backside ground her pelvis at the spectators on the far side of the upraised stage. "Down in front!" yelled another man and I turned to see a number of recognizable faces looking up at me and past: the president of the largest bank in Oak Ridge, a lawyer currently running for the Democratic nomination for Congress, and at the table beyond theirs, a dark girl all bones and starchy flesh, making conversation, as though waiting for a bus, with two deacons of the Fourth Creek Baptist church. When I glanced back at the ring of light the familiar dancer had disappeared. So I hurried after.

"Professor?" the bouncer grunted in my ear, grabbing my arm. "You know you can't do that."

"Trouble?" A sheriff's deputy stood in front of me where I landed at the end of the spin the bouncer had induced.

"I'm trying—"

"We're all trying, Professor," the bouncer said. He let go of my arm and crushed something into my palm.

"I don't want my money back," I protested. "I just have to get backstage."

"Get it on out," he said, turning me around with an easy flick of his wrist. My own wrist ached, as if from some ancient hurt, and I found myself steered toward the door as I rubbed it.

"Howdy, Professor," a uniformed sheriff's deputy said, waiting for me just outside the entrance. A car started up in the parking lot; a woman waved to me from within.

"Sorry," I said, tossing the deputy the bill and rushing toward the lot.

"Appreciate it, sir!" he called after me, the customary thank you of these parts.

I rushed over to the ditch and climbed inside my car. My hands—and my body—shook as I drove along, as though the carefully smoothed highway had become a corduroy road. If I were heading west instead of returning east, I said to myself, I'd be rolling past Kingston soon. I imagined myself climbing up, up Crab Orchard Mountain. The view there gave to the south onto the curlique, far below, of the meandering Tennessee River, silver in the sun, invisible, mostly, by night.

"Where were you?" David stood, hands on hips, at the curbside in front of the arcade.

"Where's Junie?" I said when I reached over and opened the door for him.

He jerked a thumb toward the arcade, showing me with an attempt at making mean and nasty eyes just how angry he was.

"I ran out of tokens," he said. His face looked wan and other-worldly in the parking lot lamplight.

"Is Junie still inside?"

My heart raced—I was climbing the Cumberland Plateau, that humped-up ridge that ran straight south from the Kentucky border down into Alabama. If Tennessee were an angry dog, pointing east, the plateau would be the bunched-up flesh of its neck.

"Yeah."

"Yeah?" He was climbing inside, but I held out a hand to stop him. "Yeah? How about saying, *Yes, sir*, sometimes, like some of the redneck kids do around here even when they don't know me. How about *that*?"

He was angry—I was angry. Where was Junie?

"Go get her. I don't want her in there alone!" I shouted after him.

"Yeah, *sir*!" he called to me over his shoulder, rolling his eyes up in his head, as if to show me that I was a freak and a fool, and his father only because of some error of nature.

Minutes passed. I grew nervous; my hands began to ball and quake. What if—she had been dragged from the arcade by several rough older boys who sold her to the owner of Pussycat Village? What if—she had seen me drive off, and made up her own mind to run away?

"I was in the *bath*room, Daddy," she said, climbing into the car.

"You actually *use* those bathrooms in there?"

"What was I supposed to *do*?" Junie sounded awfully close to tears, that tremulous question, quavering eyes starting back and forth between her brother and me.

"I don't know," I said, seeing canyons from the air, the rich red rocks of New Mexico, Arizona, the world as relief map, the comforting steady roar of the engines. I slapped my hands to the wheel, reached down and turned the key, and we got rolling back along the road toward Oak Ridge.

"I don't mean to make you unhappy," I said after a while, staring straight ahead where the car lamps speared the soft dark underbelly of night. "I'm thinking about a new mystery, so I got grumpy."

"Grumpy is a dwarf," Junie said.

"You're a dwarf," David said.

"David!" I warned him. We were getting closer now, speeding along Pellissippi Parkway, the fields bleeding off into the nocturnal distance. I was traveling in another plane, this one ascending from LAX, heading westward, ever westward. In six hours, Hawaii, stopover, refuel. Then into the air again, straining against the opalescent shimmer of the Pacific horizon. Here would be light such as I had never seen before, such as I had known only approximately in my earlier days when, just a few years older than David, I had been plucked from my high school in Morristown, New Jersey, and repotted at Los Alamos. The shock still reverberated in my life. My quaking hands—did they shake now because of that explosion of my youth? Did I write mysteries?

"Mom's not home," Junie declared, as though she had just been the first to reach the winning score in a board game.

"She never is," David said, in some kind of comment.

"She's got her drama group," I said.

"Yeah," he said.

"They're doing a play by an Englishman named Harold Pinter."

"So?"

"So that's what they're doing."

"Sure," he said.

"Sure, *sir*," I said.

"Sure, *sir*," he said.

"Sure, *Super*-Dad," Junie said.

"Some Super-Dad," I said.

"You are," Junie said.

"Sure," David said.

We were all staring at the dark, dark house.

THE TENNESSEE WALTZ

1

Martin

Iwas dancing with my darling when the feeling hit, and I stopped dead on my feet, Sue Beth bumping up against me just as the laws of physics describe.

"Not again, honey," she said, her usually soft voice verging on annoyance. "Sugar, we got to do something for you."

We were clinging to each other, her arms about my neck, my hands on her hips, a rock formation in the middle of the great flow of dancers at Boots 'n Saddle, a favorite cowboy bar of hers. I liked it well enough, its Cotton-Eyed Joe and mournful country songs just about perfect for the kind of mood I found myself in on Saturday nights when Arlene went out to her "drama" club and the kids ran off with their friends.

"Would you like to go?" Sue Beth, arching up on tiptoe, spoke into my ear.

From the velocity of the dancers and the density of the smoke and musk and whiskey-fog, I could tell that the night was moving along and that, if I could overcome my problem leaving might not be such a bad idea. For the past four Saturdays, while Arlene was at her "rehearsals" and Sue Beth's Andy (Andrew Jackson Goins) worked the night shift at the Telephone Company, we turned and strolled around the dance floor and then repaired to a nearby motel. My house in Oak Ridge was off limits. Even with Arlene away the kids were always in and out. The trailer that Sue Beth shared with her lineman, a tobacco-chewing, salt-and-pepper-bearded East Tennessean with a limp—and a smile, I guessed, that usually dared you to say I dare you to talk about something—that was forbidden territory. Not that Sue Beth hadn't suggested we go there the first time. I told her that it was a law of courtesy that kept me from doing that—I wouldn't befoul another man's turf—but of course it was just plain fear. I read the *News-Sentinel* every night after the *Tennessean* and the *Wall Street Journal*. I knew what deep-feeling creatures, prone as much to murder as suicide if pricked by self-doubt or a heart gone wrong, were the local caballeros.

What if Andy came home from work unexpectedly and found us together?

"You're cute," Sue Beth had told me when I finally broke down and explained why I'd rather take a motel way out in Kingston Pike.

"Oh, I am, I am," I joked with her, mind whirling about from place to place in the universe, the lab, my house, the desert where I spent my adolescence, the warm but as yet undiscovered planet where I hoped to spend my old age. Last year I had tried running away from home and that hadn't done any good—but way led on to way and the fuss made by Security led to my session, once a week, with the division psychoanalyst, who had run into personnel problems one sunny morn and hired temporary help in the person of Sue Beth Reals.

If that's not fate, then I don't know Einstein.

"You look real nervous," she'd said when I showed up for that Saturday morning session.

"I am," I told her, "nervous like I never was at my senior prom."

And I talked about New Jersey, and she mentioned dancing, and the next thing you know I was asking her to show me one of those cowboy bars some evening if both of us could get free. One or two weekends later and, just like tonight, we were parking alongside one another in the big lot behind Boots 'n Saddle and lining up to get our hands stamped at the door. I hadn't figured out too well just what I was in for—not in the way of the spectacle, that is—and had arrived sporting a string tie that Arlene had bought me many years ago in Taos and a pair of boots I usually wore only when I was mowing the lawn. Sue Beth made my heart leap a little by the care she'd put into her own costume. She had combed out her medium-length, honey-colored hair into a moderate version of the thing we used to call a ducktail, buttoned herself into a shirt with frilly collar and cuffs so white it gave back every scintilla of light it passed beneath, and eased into jeans that boldly outlined her thighs high up.

I was more nervous about stepping out (single step or two-step, whatever the rhythm turned out to be) in my own town than I'd been about pulling a Gauguin and heading without so much as a word of notice for Hereheretue, belle isle of the tropics. Who could say why? It was much more of a scandal to take off the way I did than any rumors the sight of me and Sue Beth arm in arm prancing to "Waltz Across Texas" could inspire—and who that knew me frequented a place such as Boots 'n Saddle? The head of our company? The chief of security? The FBI, CIA, NBC, CBS? I'd never been good with other people. I'd backed into romance and a marriage and family with Arlene the way I used to find my way around the streets of a big city like New York, bumped and shoved and half-pushed by others. The desert years had been the happiest, blessed by air perfect for my adolescent's skin and a welcome absence of people. I lived and ate and slept the project and nobody could get through to me who didn't work with me, and they were for the most part odd ducks like myself, all of them older but all of them, like me, or at least the way I used to be, most cheerful when thinking about numbers, alone in a room or under the sky.

Sue Beth said she wanted to hear about what I used to do and I was willing to drink Irish coffee and talk as a way of calming myself down. So I told her about all that—I thought that I might as well have been describing the adolescence of a Martian as far as she was concerned, her own life was so different. But somehow she understood the problem it led up to, the sensation that I was an intern on call from another dimension. She'd learned about moments like that by growing up with her preacher "Daddy," as she called him in the familiar tone that we Yankees give up after our first hairs sprout on our chins and elsewhere. Reverend Reals was a man who had always claimed to have been in touch with the Ancient of Days. Though he had gone to his rest fairly early in her life, when Sue Beth was just budding in the chest and getting itchy around boys, hundred of sinners had felt his touch as he brusquely shoved them beneath the sluggish waters of the Hiwassee. But for each one he'd baptized he'd apparently taken their sins on his shoulders, or in his liver, to be exact, tipping back a cup and then another and another of homemade corn liquor when they were first starting out. During the successful years, when boys in the Kinney community with bulging muscles and their hands in their coveralls sidled up to Sue Beth, the preacher's daughter, as though she might have been royalty, he switched to Jack Daniels.

At his funeral, a stringy-haired woman in a pale blue dress showed up and told the assembled family members that she was going to fight them for the possession of the estate.

"There weren't none," Sue Beth explained to me, "but he'd been keeping her all those years by telling her that he was investing money in stocks that was bound to build up and make him rich in his old age. Men! Oh, Lordy! I'm so glad I'm with you tonight, honey, instead of one of them go-rillas I growed up with."

"I'm still a man," I said, sweat pouring down my sides.

"I know, and I'm going to teach you the two-step."

And she did.

When it got to be that time on this one particular evening, multitudes sang along with the establishment's theme as it poured out of the loud speakers: "I got the boots 'n you got the saddle." The chill settled upon our sweating necks and arms and we shivered in the parking lot.

"There's another dance we're doing," I said as I opened the passenger door and watched her, slightly astonished, slide onto the seat.

"What's that, sugar?" Sue Beth, a smile on her narrow painted lips, walked spidery fingers along my shoulder.

"I used to hear it on the radio all the time when I was in New Mexico," I said. "I can't remember the name of the singer, but the song was called 'The Tennessee Waltz.' "

"Piggy Lee," she said.

"Who?" I said.

"Piggy Lee," she said.

"You mean *Peggy?*"

"That's what I said. Piggy. Piggy Lee."

"Here piggy piggy," I said, crooking my finger. "It was Patti Page."

"You making fun of me?" Her mouth opened into an almost perfect O.

"I'm *having* fun," I said. "And it's been so long I can hardly remember that it's not supposed to hurt."

The little death, the French call it, and it felt that way again this latest time. My heart was luffing like a hawk caught in a crosswind. This was supposed to soothe me, I told myself as I drove Sue Beth back to the dance hall parking lot, so why does it throw me into such quantum despond?

"You know what?" Sue Beth said with a sigh, as though she somehow understood even after disengaging from me the deep sadness I felt at the awareness of my own particles, waltzing, whirling, in time to some music whistled by a God or cosmic band with flute and Jew's harp, some country music combo of the cosmos ever mourning the impending divorce among all the matter in the universe.

"What's that?" I heard my voice as flat and uncaring as ever, the way I spoke to Arlene, the way that led me to catch myself when I spoke to the kids. "Sugar," I added. "Sugar, sugar."

"Sugar . . . ," She snuggled close to me, the way my daughter did when she was very young. "Sugar, I'm craving one of them doughnuts."

Here was our famous local doughnut, its factory and coffee shop on the corner coming up. Here we stopped and dunked our Krispy Kremes into our coffees. Here we lingered, as was appropriate, animals dreamy if not sad in the wake of our coupling, seeking immediate replenishment of the sugar we had expended in our haste.

I drove the rest of the way to the parking lot without fear of coming apart. But as soon as we rolled over the lip of the entrance Sue Beth shrieked and grabbed the wheel.

"Don't stop!" she yelled—hollered might be more exact. "Keep goin', it's Andy; he's standing right there by that car over there, keep goin'!"

"Was he armed?" I inquired as I turned and rolled us right out of the lot again.

"The ugly go-rilla was standing there talking to a little girl!"

"He'll get in trouble with the police that way," I said, steering us back up the street toward the doughnut shop.

"He's in trouble all right! We're all in trouble. Oh, Lordy," and her voice cracked.

"I thought he was supposed to be working on Saturday nights," I said, feeling the wind without opening a window. My legs trembled and my arms shook even as I held the wheel on a newly paved road.

"That's what he told me," Sue Beth said, "but looks like he's been out sneaking around with some teenage girl. And he always told me, too, he don't like to come to the dance hall because of his leg."

"His leg?"

"His limp. Pull up here," she said, and I turned into the Krispy Kreme parking lot once more.

"Would you like another doughnut?"

"At a time like this? When I just discovered the go-rilla I'm living with is a cheater?"

"Why not?"

"Would it do me good?"

"Nothing can hurt you any more," I said.

"Who you think I am? Piggy Lee?"

I hugged her right then and there.

"You made a pun, didn't you?"

"Did I? I guess I did."

A few minutes later I deposited Sue Beth back at the parking lot which was safe now, with her gorilla apparently gone off with the girl. On the drive back to Oak Ridge, rolling past mile after mile of kudzu vine still growing in the dark despite the onset of autumn, I heard Simon and Garfunkel sing "Scarborough Fair" on the radio. And I wept because I couldn't go with them. I had a project in the lab that I had to finish—or it must finish me—and hungers that kept me rummaging about the town, and nothing Arlene or the kids, who were spending the night with friends, as it turned out, nothing they could still. One day the entire earth might be covered with nothing but water and desert and kudzu. Remember me to one who lives there.

2

Andy

All the songs you hear as a boy out in the country, they tell you there's nothing so lonesome as a train whistle blowing in the night. But I think that's got to change. I left work early—unusual, but my stomach was kicking hell out of me. Something I ate, maybe, but probably something I was chewing. It was a Co-Cola I drank along with a little pinch of Red Man and a dash of the good white powder my friend Dewey brung back from a roofing job he done for a rich kid out in Sequoyah. Supposed to clear out your head, but what it did for me after the clearing, like somebody set a bomb under that roof, was everything caved in on top of me. My stomach started kicking like hell. So I come back. And like I was saying about lonesome, it used to be the train whistle in the night, but the new lonesome, *lonesome for our time,* like they might say on the television, is walking into the trailer expecting to find the best gal you ever had sitting up in front of the television waiting for you wearing nothing but one of her shortest nightgowns, a glass of whiskey in her hand, a smile on her face, that look in her eyes, and your own glass set right there on the table where she's got her pretty feet all propped up, waiting for you to pour yourself a taste—and, instead you find "Love Boat" showing on the screen with nobody watching, the sound way down, a half-filled cup of coffee on the kitchen table, a few ants enjoying themselves with a bit of crumbled Twinkies on the counter, smell of cigarettes and whiskey on the air.

I went right into the bedroom, and my heart sunk like a tire iron in Loudon Lake. There was a depression at the end of the bed big enough for Sue Beth's sweet behind, the odor of her perfume, honeysuckle, and along with her, gone is also her best cowgirl dancing clothes.

"Well, shee-it," a voice says in my ear. "Shee-it."

"And your Wichita lineman, is still on the line," was going through my head while I was driving to the dance hall, don't know why; well, I do, because I'm a lineman and she likes Glen Campbell, and I guess, well, I figure she's stringing me along and the way my heart feels, all swole up, I might as well be the fellow in the song. I pass motel after motel on the way down the Pike, and hamburger joints, and some movie theaters, and more motels, more motels, and Saturday night when I'm working overtime I never think about what the rest of the world is doing; but tonight here I am driving past these places, and I know that everybody is drinking and eating and making love while I'm just passing by, my stomach one hell of a party.

Who is she to be running off like that? Who is she? I give her what I do, help her make her car payments and fix up the trailer! She quit her job as ticket taker, I help her get through. She quit her job in the supermarket, I help her get through. She takes the job at the doctor's office and keeps on working, and you think I never did help her when she needed me. The doctor's office. The doctor?

I know her. She's a sweet thing, but she also got a big pull for money. And I can't go up against no doctor and hold my own. Not when it comes to money.

Boots 'n Saddle

There's the sign, and the parking lot as full as I ever seen it. Her car ain't nowhere in sight, but then I can't go looking through the whole lot when I got to go inside and find her in the flesh.

And her Daddy was a preacher.

Who knows what she wants? I'll bet she sure don't.

The way things has changed since I was a boy, and that wasn't all that long ago.

What's that there psychiatrist's name?

"Good evenin'."

"Howdy."

"That'll be two dollars. I need to stamp your hand."

I held out my paw to the gal with the ink stamp, trying to look past her into the dark insides of the hall.

"You seen a pretty blonde, hair all frizzed up, wearing probably a white cowgirl blouse or something and tight jeans? Oh, shee-it!" Bad enough I got this bum leg and I have to go put it in my mouth besides! There must have been a hundred and fifty-two thousand of blondes dressed like that, and the gal with the ink stamp gives me a look that tells me I sure ought to know something as simple as that. So I didn't say nothing else and hurried inside and went right up to the bar.

"Stranger?" There's this big guy with glasses under a Stetson serving up the drinks.

I ordered him to pour me a Jack Black. The music started up real loud just then. Willie Nelson, "Bloody Mary Morning." "Willie!" people was yelling, "Willie!" like he was playing live in the place instead of just on a record. I drank up and bought a few more, watching the crowd pouring round the dance floor, seeing nobody I knew, a lot of things out of the past flying through my mind like I was a drowning man, and wondering at the same time if these other sons-abitches at the bar looking so cool, if this bartender with his fancy eyeglasses and his Stetson trying to act city and cowboy at the same time, wondering if they could tell I was feeling low and lonesome? I had got Daddy in my mind, watching him waving goodbye or hello, picturing him in the door frame of the house on Crab Orchard Mountain. I never

knew if he was coming in the door or leaving on his rig—
and the train calling up from the valley, my stomach churning, remembering how many times he took me up on his
knee and told me the story about how when he went west
with his folks in the dust storms and got to California and
ate the leavings from the fields and the garbage cans and how
they must have fixed him up so bad that he had got bad blood
and he passed it along to me by way of my one leg shorter
than the other.

"Stranger?" the bartender said.

"I had enough of these by now I should be your friend."

Now where was I? Daddy, I was remembering. And he's
gone now, and how he'd whoop and holler if he could see
me a lineman, regular check, my own little pickup. Of course
this Mister Jack Daniels is helping me to forget for a second
that because of my leg I'm not up and dancing like the rest
of those hairy, horny creatures out on the floor and that Sue
Beth was fixing to leave me while I was heading out to work.

"*Friend,*" the bartender says to me, "have one of these,"
and he slides his knuckles up to my glass and shows me the
little red pill he's hiding underneath like the pea in a shell
game.

"You know, buddy," I said, after I picked it up and
popped it, "you're a lucky fellow, because something got
into my head to take your glasses off and feed 'em to you
lens by lens."

"*Friend,*" he said, "why'd you want to go and do that?"

"'Cause you're mule shit," I said, feeling this whooping
ball of hate drive up out of my aching stomach into my chest
and throat.

"On the house," the bartender said, without a crinkle in
his cool way of talking, and he knuckled another red one
over to me.

Everybody was singing, "*I got the boots 'n you got the
saddle.*"

Next thing I know this little bitty woman—perfect body,
hear this, just little, kind of like a doll-size female—comes
right up to where I'm sitting. I acted real surprised, like
nobody had ever done that before.

"Come on, you big hunk," she said, looking me straight between the eyes.

I didn't know whether it was me or Jack D. or the reds talking, but I heard someone using my voice say, "Sure do 'preciate it, but I'd just like to take you home."

Usual I'm not so bold. When I first got to meet Sue Beth it took me about two times before I even tried to do more than kiss her, though once we got past that everything went real fast. So I didn't know what would happen next. She kept on staring and staring, like she wanted to recognize somebody inside of me—and a friend instead of a stranger—before she'd talk again.

"Well . . . awright," she said, like I was the second prize she won when she really wanted a big stuffed panda bear.

"Does your momma know you're out this late?" I said to her when we got to the parking lot. I was trying not to limp and be real charming and make her laugh, because I was flying high inside.

She swung quick and hard, leaving me with a stinging jaw. I pulled back and slapped her in the head—she was so low I missed her face—and she bumped up against a car and dropped her keys. We got down on our knees to look for them and she started laughing, laughing.

"What's the joke, sugar?" I said.

And she looked up at me from where she was kneeling shoulder-high alongside me and said, "Looks like a dang prayer meeting, don't you think, Mr. Cool Hand Luke?"

3

Sue Beth

I was laying in the dark waiting for Andy to come on back, thinking about where I been, where I want to go, listening to the whistle of the L & N freight rumbling in from Nashville and then I must have dreamed because the next thing I knew I was sitting up in bed, feeling around in the empty place where Andy should have been and remembering that I had seen the woman in the blue dress rising up out of the waters of the Hiwassee, and she had a big grin on her face and I saw Daddy, his ugly big-nosed smile lighting up the world, and he anointed her a second time with the waters of the slow-flowing river, the same dream pretty much I had on and off for years now, and then Momma reaching out to me across the stream, and she's saying, "Little lamby, the Lord gave you feet to dance and Piggy Lee to sing with," and I blushed all over—this being a new part of the dream, I just didn't know it was coming—and the woman in blue was standing there at my side, and she handed me a kerchief and I dabbed at little spots of blood on my knees and my ankles, all this talk about sinning in a dream of old-timey washing away of sins. I was trying to ponder on it when the sun come bright smack through the window of the trailer and I got up real slow, wishing I'd a brought some of them Krispy Kremes home with me instead of eating two more while waiting for Andy to leave the parking lot. The handsomest preacher was on the TV, his hair all blowed dry like Farrah Fawcett's, and I was thinking what Daddy would have looked like if he'd a lived long enough; and the next thing I know Andy comes through the door, smelling like he spent the night in a barrel of fish and tobacco juice.

"Lordy," he said in a moan like a hurt dog.

"How you like 'em?" I heard myself asking him.

"Like what?" He held both hands to his head, like he was trying to keep it from falling into two pieces. His shirt was tore and he had a scratch like from a child or an animal along his right cheek.

"Your eggs," I said.

He looked at me like he was trying to decide whether to kill me or kiss me, and I gave him the same look back, figuring that if we both was to be true to what we said we believed in he would turn right around and walk out the door and I would pack and go my own way, and the only thing left in this God-forsook trailer would be the eggs frying in the skillet alongside the curling bacon, and the preacher with movie star's hair working his mouth without sound, alone, all alone on the screen that you could hardly see now because of the angle of the light coming in the window. Sometimes it seems like our lives was made of trying to be music, but nobody was singing now.

GARDEN OF THE GODS

At exactly twelve-fifteen on that Friday, the staff car, an obtrusive blue against the pale and nearly cloudless sky, pulled up to the front walk of the large L-shaped ranch house that stood on the edge of what appeared to be a field stretching endlessly eastward. The driver, dressed in uniform blues, yanked himself from his seat and stepped out onto the road. He quickly opened the rear door for his passenger, an older man not nearly as tall as he, with three stars on the shoulders of his blouse and a walk which, by itself, would have been enough for an observer, perhaps even someone besides a family member or another officer, to have easily guessed his rank.

The general was no more than halfway down the walk when the driver, who had apparently trotted into the house by way of the garage, jogged out of the cool shadows of the kitchen (cheered on by the head chef, a gawky fellow wearing a short-sleeved shirt, dark bow tie and dark trousers), passed through the foyer and arrived at the front door in time to pull it open and receive in his outstretched hand the officer's neatly deposited service cap.

"Good time," said a slightly overweight young man in his mid-twenties who, at the officer's approach, had retreated from his vantage point at the front door to the haven of the living room sofa. Except for his hair, which

was long enough to cover his ears, and his excess pound-
age, he might have passed for a younger version of the
general.

"Jamie?" The general squinted into the living room from
the foyer, his eyes still unaccustomed to the shade. "When
did you get here?"

"About two hours ago. I thought I'd surprise you."

"You haven't. You're already raising a dust storm."

The general stepped into the room and greeted his son
with outstretched hand.

"Sir?"

The younger man pushed himself off from the sofa and
shook his father's hand.

"Your crack about Smitty taking my hat."

"Well."

"Well, nothing. He's a darn good aide." The general's eyes
matched his uniform. His teeth were white as cloud.
"Where's Maisy?"

"If this is Friday, it must be charity. I understand that she's
down at the clinic."

"Community service is what we call it. Since it's Friday,
I have an operations meeting in an hour. Let's have lunch."

The two of them sat down at opposite ends of the smaller
of two tables in the dining room, the general slapping his
napkin open across his sharply creased uniform trousers, his
son unfolding his over the knees of faded blue jeans. The
gangly man who ran the kitchen entered the room bearing
a tray on which rested two steaming bowls of soup.

"Sergeant," the general said, "do you remember my son
Jamie? He'll be eating in Mrs. Evanston's place today."

"Howdy, Sergeant," Jamie said. "We met when I arrived,
Dad. He knows that Maisy isn't coming home for lunch."

"Very efficient of you two to work it out." The general
surveyed his soup. "Duck?"

"Mock turtle, sir."

"Fouled me."

"Yes, sir." The sergeant laughed dutifully and left the
room.

Jamie fingered the rim of his spoon.

"Dad, aren't you even going to ask me what I'm doing here?"

"I thought that we might enjoy our lunch first."

"It doesn't have to be the same old story, although I can tell that's what you're thinking."

"The last time it was a pretty disgusting story."

"I didn't come here to debate with you this time, Dad."

"Is debate what you call what we did? The law school must do better than that, son."

"Look, Dad . . ."

Jamie bowed his head. It appeared as though he were either praying, or brooding.

"Sandwiches, sir." The tall sergeant had padded back into the room.

"Thank you, Peterson," the general said, his voice subdued as he noticed the square, toasted sections of bread on the tray his aide deftly deposited between them.

"Your idea?" His eyes came to rest on his son's face. "Cuteness is not a quality I admire in a man."

"I came here to talk about Mom. It reminded me that I liked the lunch she fixed."

The general reached for his water glass. He took a long drink and dabbed his narrow lips with his napkin.

"What's the problem?"

"She still has the same old problem, Dad. It's the place that's changing."

"Of course I haven't seen it recently. But it's a perfectly adequate place. I get reports about it once a year, the staff, the food, the medical. . . ." The general looked toward the door.

"Everything all right, General?"

"First-class toasted cheese, Sergeant. We'll put it right up there with your coq au vin and roulages. Coffee now, if you don't mind."

"Yes, sir," the sergeant said, allowing himself a smile as he retreated from the room.

"Peterson went to cooking school in Paris when we were over at NATO," the general said.

"I guess you'd told me that once before," Jamie said, "so I knew he could swing Mom's special toasted cheese squares." He hadn't eaten any. Neither of them had eaten any.

"Look, Dad."

"I'm looking."

He looked at his watch.

Jamie was caught in the tides of a long and discomfiting meditation when he heard the car pull up to the house. He blinked hard, rose from the soft chair in the corner of the guest room at the far end of the L, and stretched as if to touch one of the fake exposed beams several feet above his head. When he pressed the "Receive" button on the speaker to the left of the door, he heard faint voices from the other side of the house. Pushing the button marked "Speak," he leaned his mouth close to the small grill in the wall and said, "Hello, Maisy."

He released the button. Moments later he heard the rustling of clothes at the upper end of the thickly carpeted hallway.

"Surprise," he said, stepping out of his room.

The tanned woman with closely cut, straw-blonde hair and a long, wolflike face stood as still as if she had encountered a snake or a chuckhole on the path in front of her. Her dark blue nurse's uniform contrasted oddly with the faint look of annoyance that passed across her face.

"Jamie! Sergeant Peterson told me you were here. He said that you'd ordered toasted cheese sandwiches for your lunch with Bill. As the children at the well-baby clinic say, 'Yuck!' "

Jamie tried hard to keep from smiling.

"It's a terrific meal for a kid, Maisy. I never want to get so jaded that I can't enjoy a good cheese sandwich."

"Why, of course not," the woman said. "And . . . speaking of enjoyment, why don't you march out to the bar and fix us both a drink while I change out of this uniform?"

"Vodka and lime juice?"

"You remembered. Dear boy. Yes. See you in a jif."

He walked up the hall toward the living room, taking the time to study the familiar framed photographs on the walls, his father in various uniforms—flight suit, parade uniform, dress whites, and the football suit bearing the markings of his home state university, the very place where Jamie now studied, that he last wore when he was several years younger than Jamie was now—and saying under his breath as he walked, " 'See you in a jif . . . see you in a jif . . . !' "

"You're looking quite well," Maisy said just as he returned from the bar. She was wearing a brown wool sweater suit, stockings, and low-heeled shoes that strapped around her ankles. They sat together, glasses in hand, on the sofa in front of the living room picture window. There was still snow on the highest peak. The lesser mountains, though no low hills themselves, were bundled merely in white haze and cloud.

"I'd bet you say that to all the babies in the clinic," Jamie said. "You're looking well yourself."

"Thank you." She took a long swallow from her glass. "I run with Bill every morning. It's awfully difficult to find a good tennis partner around here. All the best women are either going to school or endlessly pushing prams. Did you bring tennis gear? Sergeant Peterson said that he didn't see you carry in any luggage."

"Don't worry, Maisy. I'm not staying long."

She pretended that she hadn't heard this last remark. "Did you drive? I didn't notice an extra car out front."

"I flew to Denver and took the bus down."

"Why didn't you fly directly here instead of taking the awful bus? It's not one of your new protests, is it?"

He ignored her remark this time.

"I missed my connection. All I could get on short notice was a light plane. I didn't want to fly a light plane."

"Don't let your father hear that."

"He won't, unless you tell him."

"You can trust me."

She glanced over her shoulder at the mountains. Jamie followed her gaze to see the sun, elongated and deeply red, an Easter egg, pressed against the mountains by a giant palm.

"It must be beautiful right now in the Garden of the Gods, don't you think?"

"I didn't get around to see it the first time I was here," Jamie said, still clenching his glass in his fist.

"I forgot. It wasn't under the most propitious circumstances, your last visit, was it? But this time you've got to stay long enough to see the Garden, and the zoo, and the Broadmoor—don't forget our famous hotel. Perhaps your father might even show the inside of his command post, if it seems like the correct thing. . . ."

Jamie was only half-listening while he watched the western horizon as many-colored streaks of light speared up beyond the mountains, smeary but beautiful, like the artwork of a gifted child.

"You're not here to make more trouble, are you?" Maisy was saying. "Your father is under enormous pressure, and he's only just *barely* forgotten about the last episode in your little saga. Can you tell me what you're up to, Jamie? I mean, aside from enjoying a visit with your family."

Jamie cleared his throat as though about to speak. But some pressure kept his lips closed, and then Sergeant Peterson padded up to them through the gathering shadows of the large high-ceilinged room.

"Telephone, Mrs. Evanston."

"I didn't even hear it ring. Jamie?"

"You're excused."

She nodded, rising and following the tall man from the room.

Her image remained in the form of a bland, creamy portrait on the far wall which Jamie had not noticed until now. She wore a pearl necklace at her throat and a reassuring look on her narrow face. Her hair was long, unlike its present length which left her ears exposed. He had seen a photograph of her father once in a history of World War One— she had inherited the jaw, and the ears. His own father glowered from the frame alongside her, her second general, his eyes bullet-grey, his teeth masked by his determined lips.

The paintings were not the only articles in the room which he didn't recognize. The large, blue-jacketed Bible that lay open on the table at his end of the sofa was an old one, but he hadn't seen it before. He lifted it, and thumped it with his palm. Picking through its thin, delicate pages, he found that because of the fading of the light he was unable to read more than the boldest captions—*Genesis, Exodus,*

Matthew. He turned back to the inside front cover for a glimpse of a family name, his own or that of Maisy's. But there was none, or at least he found none before his step-mother stepped back into the room.

"Jamie, will you fix me another?"

"At your service."

He set the book down on the end table and got up and went to the bar at the kitchen side of the dining room. He needed light to make the drinks by. When he returned to the living room Maisy had switched on several floor lamps, and their glare diminished the view of the mountains and the thickening blue of the sky.

"Cheers," she said, dipping her glass slightly toward him.

"Cheers," said Jamie.

"Is it money?" she asked. "You can speak frankly."

"Not money for me. I do quite well, thank you, on what I saved working the pipeline."

"For your mother then?"

She turned her head alertly, as though she heard the buzzing of an insect, or a distant bell.

It was the sergeant again, stalking across the thick carpet.

"Mrs. Evanston?"

"Yes, Sergeant?"

"I've checked. We'll be fine."

"Thank you."

"Yes, ma'am."

The sergeant left the room as quietly as he had arrived.

"Your father called, Jamie. A congressional subcommittee has just come to town. He thought we'd better have the chairman over for dinner this evening."

"Shit."

"*Really,* Jamie!"

"I wanted to have some time to talk with him tonight. He gave me about five minutes at lunch before he drove off to a meeting."

Something flickered across her face, as though one of the lamps had briefly short-circuited and left them in darkness for just a fleeting moment and then flashed back into service.

"He does have his duty."

"He hasn't seen me face to face for nearly two years and he invites some visiting congressman over for dinner?"

"I'm sure you'll be able to talk after we eat. No one stays up very late around here. The air, you know. Perhaps there's a cheerful side to this. Perhaps now we can persuade you to stay awhile."

Jamie studied the portraits on the wall as he swallowed some of his drink.

"May I borrow your car?"

"Of course, but we're going to sit down at eight—"

"I'm not eating, Maisy."

"He won't like that. If one is going to ask favors of him, one doesn't start off by refusing to dine with him."

"The altitude's getting me. The air, you know. Please let me have the keys." He held out his empty hand.

"If you're really ill, dear boy, perhaps you shouldn't . . . Oh, I see. Well, they're in the ignition. But won't you try to get back in time for dessert?"

Jamie placed his glass on the thick cover of the Bible and stood up.

"I don't think so."

"You ought to at least consider running with us in the morning. It's a good time to speak to Bill; he's very alert then and not yet got his head filled with thoughts of aircraft and radars. I'll put an alarm clock in your room and set it for five, bright and early, when we do our miles through the sagebrush."

"I'll consider it. I think I'm going to leave in the morning."

"For your mother's sake, run with us."

She grasped her glass and swallowed all the liquid covering the ice.

When Jamie climbed into Maisy's little British sedan and started it up, the sky had turned as inky-blue as the cover of the Bible on the end table. By the time he left the air base and drove west along the highway, darkness framed the floating lights of oncoming vehicles and neon signs of motels and hamburger and taco stands. His father's staff car was undoubtedly rolling homeward at this very moment, the old man enthroned in the backseat reading a report, or another

Bible, under the stern, intense beam of a Tensor lamp. He imagined for an instant swerving headlong into those lights. It would end their agony if he did, but it would only make his mother's worse, he thought.

He thought of her as he reached the central square, a place where old Mexicans and cowboys had once gathered, and made a right turn onto a road leading northward and away from the broad main city streets. Though two time zones away, he could still feel her as though she were sitting in the seat alongside him. Night had draped the grounds for hours now, though she probably still huddled at the window admiring the budding maples and the dying elms. In the hall, strangers shuffled back and forth like zombies in a Hollywood film of the forties.

He flicked the radio on, catching a burst of static, a bit of western blues, resonant steel guitars, and flicked it off again. He was already lost. A giant plastic steer with horns as long as a man's body loomed in the distance, announcing char-broiled steaks. A gas station lay just beyond it. Jamie pulled in to ask directions.

"Har-deen?" The attendant was a mustachioed old man with little English. "No say, no say."

Jamie's stomach growled. The car rumbled around him. He pulled away from the gas pump to a place beneath a lamp-post and attempted to open the glove compartment. It was locked, and so he had to turn off the ignition and withdraw the key in order to free the key ring. He was hoping to find a map. As he yanked open the door to the compartment a large opaque bottle rolled into his hand.

"Well, well."

He unscrewed the top, sniffed the contents, and took a long pull from the bottle. I won't give in, he told himself, taking another drink before hugging the bottle to his chest, capping it, and returning it to the glove compartment. Instead of turning back toward the sign of the plastic longhorn, he drove on.

Garden of the Gods. His daring was repaid by the sight of this small white signpost directing him to make a left turn at the next corner. Soon he found himself bouncing along a dark, unpaved road. Moths as large as birds fluttered in front of the windshield. A jackrabbit sat in the middle of the road. Jamie flicked his bright lamps at the hypnotized creature and then swerved awkwardly in order to avoid it. He made another withdrawal from the bottle. The road began to climb. A few minutes later, convinced that he had missed another crucial turn, he pulled onto the shoulder and tried to get his bearings. Rock formations illuminated by spotlights, or a hidden moon, lay far below and behind him, like some model he once made in grade school for a report on the landscape of a distant planet. He took a small capsule from his shirt pocket and washed it down with another swallow from the bottle.

Manitou Springs. The next marker convinced him that he had taken yet another wrong turn. The car's fault, he decided, studying the gas gauge, perusing the speedometer. It just kept on going. Houses flowed past him, and storefronts. After turning around in the parking lot of a dimly lighted crafts shop, he drove back in the direction in which he thought he had come. But the road looped around in a confusing way, and he noticed a signal tower winking on and off which he could have sworn had not been there when last he had looked. The city twinkled below him now as if seen from the window of a jet just at takeoff or landing. Somewhere above him loomed his father's mountain with its command post fitted into the hollow of the man-carved rock. A few quick twists of his neck, and he bore down on the wheel again, driving with great concentration.

He passed a drive-in theater, he passed cars moving the opposite direction, and then he was driving more slowly, among the trees again, on curves, and he saw stables, hillside meadows, more houses, trees. The city's grand hotel glowed through the pines like a luxury liner sighted from a great distance at sea. He kept on driving, his stomach contracting as if from hunger or airsickness. The road wound upward through the forest. After a dozen more uptending turns, Jamie stopped to urinate. Music drifted faintly through the trees, and voices, too, as if the sounds from the hotel or the drive-in theater echoed up the side of the mountain. His breath tasted unaccountably of toasted cheese. He washed his mouth with vodka and flipped the now empty bottle into the dark spaces between the trees.

So soon afterward that it seemed for a few terrifying seconds that he might have disturbed some sleeping monster of the upper woods, a murderous shriek echoed overhead. As the wind shifted it delivered the ammoniac odor of large, soiled felines and the stench of the dung of massive land beasts—elephants, rhinos, hippos—a smell that descended upon him like a thick, old blanket dropped out of a sky as dark and tarry as a pit of prehistoric bones. He was embarrassed at his momentary fear, and then ashamed, a confused, pudgy law student leaning against his stepmother's car and trembling like a little boy. The shriek sounded again, but the outcry begun in ferocity fell away into a splintered, high-pitched squawk, more like that of a peacock than a hunting beast, though there was no way of telling—not then.

The house was dark when he returned. Not even a night-light showed through the curtains masking the inside from view, although the lawn and the building itself lay awash in the light from the lamp on the last pole in a long row of lamps that ringed the base. Jamie felt drained. The sight of a large jackrabbit nibbling at the foot of a young ash tree made him wonder where his own hunger had gone. He wanted only to sleep, and he quietly retreated to the car and fetched the keys from the dashboard so that he could unlock the front door. At his approach, the rabbit leaped into the darkness beyond the last lamp.

The door was troublesome. It took some jiggling and wrenching to work it open despite the key, and Jamie was annoyed at himself for making even the smallest sounds. He was halfway down the hall when he noticed the light beneath the door to the master bedroom. He got as far as the photograph of his father standing in front of the wing of his last fighter plane when he heard the voices.

"Who art in Heaven," the general said.

"Who art in Heaven," his stepmother in a schoolgirl's voice repeated after him.

"Hallowed be thy Name." The general.

"Hallowed be thy Name." Maisy.

"Thy Kingdom Come." The general.

"Thy Kingdom Come." Maisy.

"Thy Will be Done." The general.

"Thy Will be Done." Maisy.

Jamie hurried past the door and into his own room near the end of the L. He stripped to his undershorts and climbed into bed. A strange sound sat him up almost at once. Certain that it came from outside, he leaped to the window and saw the largest jackrabbit in the world poised mutely on its hind paws, its eyes fixed on the house. Jamie rapped on the glass. The rabbit blinked twice, as if sending code, and sprung away into the dark field.

At the sound of the alarm, he slid out of bed and used the bathroom. Maisy had set out several pairs of shorts and running shoes. The shoes were not a problem—he and his father wore the same size. But all of the shorts were too tight. He considered for a moment running in his undershorts, but decided to put on his jeans instead.

Maisy lay on the living room rug doing push-ups in front of the dark picture window. She was dressed like a young tennis player, her long white legs lean and solid, marked only here and there with thin blue veins, and she gave off the scent of expensive perfume and fresh toothpaste that contrasted sharply with the bitter odors and tastes of his own body and mouth.

"Where's Bill?" he asked.

"Already running."

Jamie flopped down on the rug a few feet from her and performed a series of inept push-ups. His own grunting sounded a heavy counterpoint to his stepmother's puffs and sighs.

"Hup!"

She leaped to her feet, and he did the same, following her out of the house and breaking into a jog alongside her. The air was chilly for the season—altitude, he remembered—and he was glad when he noticed the gooseflesh rippling along Maisy's thin arms that he had worn his shirt and long pants.

"How far?"

"Does he run? Five miles. You don't have to. Go all the way."

The two of them sounded to Jamie like a pair of ponies as they clopped along the street and onto the lawn that led to the edge of the endless field. There was no moon, only a few stars. He could see nothing ahead but the outline of a hillock rising up to meet them as their feet hit the loose, pebbly ground beyond the grass.

"Stay on the path," Maisy said. "You could break a leg. If you step into a chuckhole."

"Would he shoot me?"

"He might." It was still too dark to see her face, but he could tell that she was smiling.

"I believe it."

"Oh, Jamie."

"Oh, baby doo-doo! Does he expect us to catch up with him?"

"The trail circles back. But it would be nice."

"You mean, he wants me to?"

"It would be nice."

A twinge in his left side caught Jamie off guard. He made a noise. His stepmother glanced back at him over her shoulder.

"You okay?"

"I should lose some weight."

She slowed down and he came even with her.

"We all should."

"Not you."

"Thanks."

"You're welcome. Jolly big cactus, that."

"I didn't notice."

"Too late. Keep on."

There was a trickle of light in the east now, enough to reveal that what Jamie had taken for the horizon was actually a bank of clouds. He lowered his sights and noticed a figure all in white pounding over the rise.

"Dad?" he called.

"Mornin'!"

The man charged past them, huffing as he ran.

"Colonel from next street," Maisy said. "Can't remember his name."

"Running. . . ."

"What?"

"Running, our secret weapon."

Jamie clutched his aching side.

"Come on, Yank!" Maisy urged him to the top of the rise. The cool air in his nostrils, the sharp, brittle smell from of the field distracted him from an ache in his lungs. The path leveled off and turned southward along a little gully and it was suddenly dark again, as though they had trotted backward in time. Huff, and foot, huff, and foot. When he looked up again, he picked out a streak of light high to the east, a jet trail that had caught the first hint of sun.

Maisy had gotten far ahead of him, and as he plodded along where the path turned eastward onto higher ground, she doubled back.

"I can't," he said as she came alongside him.

"You must, Jamie. It's the only way. For Helen's sake."

"Helen? I'll try."

He charged after her, his lungs flaring up like paper logs. He could see sagebrush now, and row after row of low bushes, small cactus between, as though this wilderness had been planted by a hand to fit some plan. A covey of tiny birds blew up at their approach, like fish in the wake of a stone or a swimmer. He watched them veer toward the dark part of the sky, and felt his right foot twist beneath him as he took his next forward step and sent himself vaulting head downward into the brush.

"Break anything?"

Maisy stood over him, hands on hips, her small chest heaving as rapidly as though she wore a bird's heart within.

He shook his aching head.

"Damn you, Jamie! You should have come for dinner!"

She offered him her hand.

He was surprised at her language but not at the look on her face which he was sure she reserved for recalcitrant servants, naughty children, and those she defeated at tennis. Above her the darkness had leached away until the sky was now a deep but penetrable underwater blue. A few small clouds hovered far above the manufacturing of the dawn.

"Come on," she said, as annoyed as he had ever heard her.

"I'll wait here." He stared at her knees. "You catch up with him and explain that *Helen* has to have a better place to stay in."

"What? Not me, pal." She replaced her hand on her hip. "I'm not sticking my nose into this one. I've done all I'm going to do trying to arrange this little marathon."

In the growing light, he could see the soak gathering beneath her armpits and at the cleft of her shirt. From this angle he could see the space between her shorts and her thin-veined upper thigh to a point just below the leg band of her silky underpants.

"It's your goddamn money, Maisy. We all know that."

"Jamie, that's a ghastly thing to say. I'm not going to honor such statements with a reply." She turned, poised on the toe of one running shoe.

"Talk to him, Maisy. Catch up with him and talk."

She kicked pebbles to the side of the path, painstakingly, like a little girl lost in play.

"As a matter of fact, I already did. Last night after dinner, when you should have been there. He says that your mother is perfectly fine where she is."

"The place is a zoo, Maisy. Talk to him again."

"Why should I? Give me one good reason why I should."

He fingered the grainy soil. The throbbing in his head subsided enough for him to appreciate the pain in his ankle.

"Because I found your bottle in the glove compartment."

"Oh, Christ!"

She turned and started running up the path.

He could see that it was truly becoming light now. Clouds stippled with colors like layers of various minerals dominated the horizon. It was cold on the pebbly path where he lay, and he hugged his knees for warmth, after a few minutes swiveling around as if on call to see what had happened behind him. It was one of those moments when light confounds geography—it could either be the last part of the day or the first part of morning, and west east, east west. The tallest mountain on the horizon rose out of a sea of clouds as it might have when the burning earth first buckled and served up rocky peaks, but silently, as though in a film that had lost its soundtrack. Closer at hand, a fat green lizard peeped out at him from beneath a cover of crusty leaves, its eyes two starry points of light. A thick-armored beetle scuttled tanklike past his fingers, and then stopped, and then moved again, and then stopped. Together they waited for the runners to return.

ON THE TRAM

Calif ornia was nearly two
states behind them when Kann told her that he had forgotten to buy the gift.

"How could you have forgotten," Marion said. "You've had only about seven months to think about what you wanted to bring her."

"I was thinking about it," he said, clearing his throat, "but I never could really pinpoint what I wanted to bring." He was steering with one hand and with the other consulting the map. "When do we get to Albuquerque?"

"About five o'clock." Marion was an analyst of mathematical systems as they applied to computers of vast capability—it didn't disturb her when she learned that Kann was lousy at computations such as the tax on the long distance portions of telephone bills.

An Intermountain rig as long as a dinosaur roared past them in the right-hand lane and their Japanese wagon shuddered like a child caught in a draft.

Kann gripped the wheel with great intensity. All morning the sun had poked into his eyes, but now that it filled the rear of the car with boiling air, he squinted at the slightly undulating highway ahead as though the sun had just risen. He began to blink and blink, unable to stop himself, and the landscape beyond the windshield turned into a field lighted by a stroboscopic projector, the kind he once lifted from an instruments warehouse when he was running with a band.

"Why is the car shaking?" Marion plucked at Kann's shirt-sleeve, and he came out of his trance in time to keep the vehicle from straying any further across the center line. He sniffed and listened to something within the burr and tumble of the rumbling automobile, then focused his eyes on the mesas ahead.

"We'll have to stop in Albuquerque."

Marion made a noise in her throat.

"You don't want to stop?"

"If you're tired, I'll drive."

"What about your night vision?"

"I don't like to be reminded of that."

"Your flawed cones and rods."

"Please don't read it back to me as though you've just discovered it."

"I'm trying to help. I'm slowing down. You shouldn't drive after dark—your one flaw."

"Can we please end the irony?"

Signs had begun to spring up across the desert ahead. Mountains appeared larger in the late afternoon than they had in the brighter hours. They pulled off to the side of the highway and listened, in silence broken only by the rushing pulse of passing cars and truck. The engine lugged, not a mere hint now but trouble itself.

"I thought you had the car checked out," Marion said.

"It's not what you think. I did take it in. It's something else."

"Do we need anything more?" Annoyance returned to her voice, the way the dark came on, with regularity.

"No, I was thinking," he said, as they rolled at half their normal highway speed down the long hill toward the city, "my body is here, in this car, in the desert, but my mind is still in high school."

In this world
of ordinary people . . .
He was singing in the shower.
Extra-ordinary people . . .

He was singing in the shower of the Motel Cibola, in a stall that reeked of dust and mountain pine.

I'm glad there is you.

"You're certainly cheerful for a man with a car that doesn't work," Marion called out. She had just stepped from the shower herself and was swabbing her lean, pale body with a worn white towel.

"I'm just glad. . . ." Kann turned off the water and emerged from the stall. "I'm just glad that we caught the repair place before they closed. With a little luck, we might get out of here by tomorrow afternoon."

"What duh yuh think is wruh . . ." Marion brushed her teeth, her arm working like a fiddler's. Kann inched up behind her and mugged in the steamy mirror.

"I love women who spit." He twisted his lips into one last smile and then snatched a towel from the rack. "Which reminds me. I'll call Katy."

"She spits?"

"Her mother does."

"On you."

"That was what reminded me."

"You shave. I'll make a phone call myself."

"Who are you calling? Don't bother the mechanic again. Anyway, they're closed."

"I'm just making a call. I don't even know if I can find the number."

"Mystery," Kann said. "I love mystery. I'll shave." But he didn't love mystery at all—he was lying, and he knew it. He watched her carefully fold her towel and place it upon the shelf alongside the sink, watched her in the mirror as, with a sweeping movement of breasts and arms, she left the bathroom and closed the door behind her. A year had passed since that afternoon when they had met, and he still scarcely knew her. But when he goaded himself for this he had to admit that of the thirty-five years of being himself he could say almost the same thing. He was a horribly confused and unhappy person, and yet he sang in the shower. He missed the child cleaved from him by a New Jersey judge, and yet he had not yet bought the grand gift that he had promised her when last they spoke over the telephone—if a conversation was what it might be called when tormented father spoke to a barely articulate five-year-old over lines stretched beneath the earth three thousand some miles between. As if within his nervous system there lived a demon counterpart to the already sadistic judge in Middlesex County who had awarded Katy to the woman who spat, Kann's arm came up—he watched all this in a circle he had wiped clean in the mirror a moment before—and he saw the razor and he watched his hand draw it to his throat and tear downwards at his full day's growth of beard; and he saw the blood before he felt the sting.

"You've cut yourself," Marion said when he stepped through the bathroom door. She was pulling on a pair of white slacks.

"You noticed," Kann said.

"No, seriously, Gregg, clean up that blood and get dressed. They're coming by in a few minutes." She glanced at him from beneath the curtain of jet-black hair that fell across her eyes whenever she tilted her head too far to the left.

"Who's 'they'?"

"When you were talking to the mechanic I remembered that an old friend of mine was supposed to be living in Albuquerque. So I looked him up in the phone book, and lo and behold, he was there."

"He?"

"Clean up the blood; call Katy."

"I can't wait." He touched a finger to his throat and found that the cut had dried somewhat. "Is this some kind of a television comedy? The car breaks down, now old boyfriends?"

Marion gave him her most professional look.

"It's your tone of voice that's turning this into a comedy," she said, plucking her hairbrush from her bag.

"*I don't know,*" Katy was saying in his ear when he heard the knock at the door: Half a dozen times within the last two minutes she had replied to his questions in this fashion, and Kann knew that she knew that he knew that she knew more than that.

"I'll go out and meet them," Marion called in his ear, and he nodded, listening, with his other ear to the receiver, to the expensive buzz and hum that transpired between this telephone and the one in New Jersey into whose mouthpiece his Katy was not speaking, except to tell him that she didn't know.

"Do you like comedy?" he had asked.

She gave him her customary reply.

"Because Daddy is stuck with a broken car in the middle of New Mexico—that's a far western state, but not as far west as California, because Daddy's on his way to see you. Do you remember California? When you flew out? And we went to see the sea lions?" he said.

She didn't know.

"Listen, Gregg," the other voice came on the line, *"you're torturing this little girl with your stupid questions. Get your ass in gear and come and bring her the present the way you promised. And if your car isn't working, rent another one and get on with it."*

"I wish you wouldn't eavesdrop when I'm taking to—"

"Oh, don't be a fool!"

Words clogged his throat.

"Gregg?"

Marion stuck her head in the door.

"Daddy will see you in a few days, honey," Kann said into the mouthpiece. He signaled to Marion that he was ready to depart.

"Gregg! Now you listen . . ."

The woman spat more words at him from her end of the line. He burned with shame that his daughter had to listen to the kinds of things her mother had to say to him, and his heart sank still further into the abyss of embarrassment as he set the telephone down on the night table because he guessed that Katy must listen to such language all the time. He touched a finger to his throat—the blood had dried. Before stepping out the door, he ducked back into the bathroom, dabbed at the dried scab with a wet facecloth, and after one quick and friendly grimace at the man in the glass went to join the party.

"Gregg Kann, Walter Michaels; Walter, Gregg."

Marion, her arm about the waist of the slender, red-cheeked man dressed in T-shirt and slacks the color of her own, reached for Gregg's hand. A taller, swarthier man closer to Gregg's own age stood on the other side of the door.

"I'm José Velarde," this man said in a flat, unaccented voice that contrasted with his Latin appearance.

"José," Gregg said. "Walter. So who's—?"

"He's confused," Velarde said.

"I'd be, too," Walter said.

"He just got off the telephone with his daughter," Marion said. "She's in New York, and we're on our way there for a visit."

They climbed into the Michaels-Velarde Volkswagen bug and drove out of the motel parking lot onto a main street. The sun had fallen back far to the west while Kann and Marion had been showering and dressing, and the sky appeared to have had a thin membrane of brightness torn away from it. Staring into that glow Kann felt disoriented and grabbed Marion's hand: in his mind he followed the sun back to their small house on the eastern slopes of the Santa Cruz Mountains, where it was still merely late afternoon, and then eastward, all the way to where his daughter, prisoner of the woman who spat, lay in darkness, trying now to sleep, no doubt. The velocity of these travels left him dizzy. To calm himself he listened to the talk of these old friends.

Walter, he learned, had worked across the aisle from Marion when she had arrived in Menlo Park from Michigan and had helped her find an apartment more appealing than the drab single room with kitchenette she had first inhabited. He had been living alone then, and so had she, and they had spent quite a lot of time together, cooking meals, going to the beach. It was only when the Crab came on the scene that Walter made an exit.

"The Crab?"

Kann had still been watching the sky—now he noticed the mountains that they had first seen hours ago on their approach to the city edging larger on their right, to the east.

"Sandia Peak," Velarde turned to him and said, as though he had been reading his mind.

"The Crab was John Fountain, Marion's ex—I hope she's mentioned him. Dear?" Walter stared straight ahead as he drove.

Marion nestled closer to Kann and pecked at his cheek. "Of course."

"John was what she called him, not 'the crab,' " Kann said. "That's why it didn't sound familiar. Was that his sign?"

Walter laughed.

"No, he was just a crab. No sign, no symbolism, just plain old crab, crab, crab. OK, I've forgotten about California and all you astrologers."

"Not me," Kann said. "I only work there. I haven't taken out citizenship papers yet."

"A sense of humor," Velarde said. "Does Walter threaten you?"

"José," Walter had steered them onto the highway and now he steered them off onto a secondary road that turned dusty among rust-colored hills.

"I was just asking. The way I heard the story, you threatened the Crab—"

"Later," said Walter, slowing down on the approach to what appeared to be a ramshackle restaurant on a low rise ahead. Kann then noticed the windows of the large shed beyond it and the cables of the tram leading out from under the roof and up into the rocks on the hillside. They parked and climbed the stairs to the shed, which turned out to be the tram station and the housing for red steel spindles—taller than a man, taller than an ordinary room—onto which the cable was wound and unwound with a great whirring and creaking of heavy steel lines.

"You said you were taking us to dinner, not to an amusement park," Marion said.

"Don't let the Midwest in you hide the best in you, dear." Walter took her arm and led her up to the booth where a young fellow in a blue denim trucker's cap sold tickets. About a dozen people stood waiting for the arrival of the next car, and they joined the group.

"This is adventure—an ascent up the mountain to be fed," Velarde said. "Or something biblical like that."

"Is there a souvenir shop up there?" Kann asked. "I need to buy a present for my daughter."

"Your daughter? Tell us about her," Walter said.

Kann wanted to speak, but something jammed in his windpipe. He was grateful just then for the approaching tram car that appeared above them just over the nearest rise of rocks; he took the opportunity to herd Marion and Walter and Velarde into the line that was forming at the entrance to the shed. Except for a babe in arms or two, most of the passengers were adults, couples, at least the ones making the ascent at this time of day. The cliffside ahead lay all in shadow and the little piece of sky that Kann noticed beyond it and above had turned velvet blue. The car lurched into its docking space and the attendant unlocked the door to allow another dozen or more people, mostly parents with children waist high, to exit from the tram.

"Families go down, lovers go up," Velarde said as, at the attendant's command, they stepped forward into the car.

"Aren't we poetical tonight," Walter said.

"That's why we get along so well together," Velarde said. "I'm poetry, and you're music."

Marion had Kann in tow as though he had suddenly been transformed into one of those waist-tall children. The attendant moved a lever and the car inched forward out of the dock, sliding horizontally instead of immediately upward. It wasn't until they had skimmed over the first high perch of pear-shaped rocks—as high as a house—that Kann understood the angle of their climb.

"It's like we're strung on a clothesline," he said, "and a giant mother at the top of the mountain is hauling us up."

"Do you enjoy this?" Velarde asked at Kann's elbow. "It makes me dizzy, to tell you the truth. But Walter always likes to impress visitors with the view. It was once all a great ocean here, you know."

"It's impressive," Kann said, glancing over at Walter before taking in the valley that was slowing falling away beneath them. Lights had begun to spark up in the bowl of the city, silvery reflections on the surface of a pond in sun. But the sun itself had disappeared.

"It's beautiful," Velarde said. "If you don't notice the smog. When I was growing up it was a different world here. We had no dirty air, now with all the cars and such the air has gotten bad enough to kill you."

"I guess it's all in your perspective," Kann said. "It doesn't seem so smoggy to me. You should try and breathe where I grew up."

"Where was that?" Walter sounded as interested in Kann's background as he did on the question of his daughter.

"In darkest New Jersey. Under the shadow of the chemical plants and oil refineries."

"Somebody's got to refine it," Walter said.

"Is that what you do?" Kann asked.

Walter looked at Marion.

"He used to work on rockets," she said.

"Not anymore, though."

"He's a free-lance design engineer now," Velarde said. "Who wants to work on secret projects anyhow? Not secrets that are going to blow us all up anyway."

Kann glanced down at the receding valley.

"You lost your clearance?"

"He traded it in for love," Velarde said. "Wouldn't you do the same?"

"Marion'd never have to," Walter said immediately. "She's straight as an arrow. Lived with her maiden aunt until the Crab came along. Isn't that right, darling?"

Kann watched Marion's face turn from red to a shadowy copper in the last of the fading light. He kept silent and for a moment the four of them listened to the clanking of the cable and the chatter of the others in the car. Now and then as the operator shifted gears a woman would squeal in fear, or mock-terror, sounds that reminded Kann that he ought to feel vertigo. But as they slowly rolled their way above higher and higher points of rock, he discovered that he was noticing less and less about their journey.

"Don't look back," someone said in his ear, and he turned to see that Marion and the two men had drifted to the rear of the car, leaving him surrounded by other travelers. He stared over at them and at the sky beyond the window of the car, now light above and dark below, like a glass filled with heavy dye that has drifted to the bottom of the pool of clearer fluid.

"*Gregg!*" The voice spat in his inner ear. He shivered as the car bucked and swayed at the approach to the upper station. His knees felt like water and his head swelled with fear.

It was colder up at the summit, and he was not prepared.

"I should have said something," Walter said, "but I guess I'm used to it. In late spring you can still find lots of snow up here. But you've got your big strong man to keep you warm."

"You are looking a little pale," Marion said as Kann, taking his cue from Walter, slipped his arm around her waist as they descended the steps of the tram station onto the side of the mountain itself. A sign warned them about standing too close to the edge, where loose rocks might carry the inattentive tourist over the side.

"Just hungry," he said, noticing the restaurant that lay ahead of them across a small footbridge over broken rock and the beginnings of a ravine.

Inside it was quite crowded, so many had come up the incline before them and had not yet returned.

"And you can cheat," Walter said as they stood at the noisy bar. "You can drive around to the east side of the peak and take the road up. But it's hours."

"And no adventure," Velarde said.

"Who'd want to live that way?" Kann raised his glass to the others and they in turn raised theirs to him.

Kann reached for Marion's hand. Though the restaurant was heated even at this time of year and the scores of diners added to the fever of the room, he could still feel the cold wind whipping across the surface of the peak, across the footbridge leading them here, singing, singing in the cables of the tram. He raised his glass, as if to make another toast.

They drank, and the next thing he knew a wide-hipped young waitress, with braided blond hair like vines, was leading them to their table at the window side. Marion excused herself and headed off.

"My daughter," Kann said aloud after the girl handed them menus.

"She's not *that* big," Velarde rolled his eyes at the departing girl.

"One day she'll be," Kann said.

"Oh, don't live in the future," Velarde said, waving off Kann's mock-distress with his menu. "Anyway, the future is going to be just fine for daughters. It's sons you ought to sympathize with."

"I do. I'm a son."

"I'm a moon, myself," Walter said, staring out at the mountainscape through the thick glass alongside their table.

"You mean you shoot the moon," Velarde said.

"No, I shoot the sun," Walter said. "I'm all astro-lad, or used to be."

The waitress returned to take their orders.

"Where's Marion?" Velarde said.

"In the little girls' room," Walter said.

"She's a big girl," Kann said.

"Do you want to order now or would you like to wait?" asked the young waitress with the braids like vines.

"We better wait," Walter said. "One of our party has to return."

"So tell us," Velarde said.

"Yes?" Kann looked out past the point where Walter had been gazing. "Look at that!" he said, his voice rising like an adolescent's. The other two men peered through the glass.

"It's Marion," Kann said, "she's out on the terrace."

"She better be careful, with her night vision," Walter said. "You saw the sign."

"I thought she was peeing," Velarde said.

"She must have gone out for some air," Kann said.

"For some wind," Velarde said. "At ten thousand feet air is officially wind."

Kann stood up and pushed his chair around in front of him.

"I'm going out to get her."

"Oh, let her be," Velarde said. "She's just enjoying the 'tudes, the solitude and the altitude."

"But she can't see where she's going," Walter said, his brow furrowed suddenly.

"So who can? Mr. Kann? Can you, Mr. Kann?"

"You don't need more wine, you need a muzzle," Walter said.

"You and what veteran?" Velarde said.

"Veterinarian," Walter said.

"I prefer a veteran," Velarde said.

"You've got one," Walter said.

"A real one," Velarde said. "What war have you been through?"

"The battle of my bulge."

In order to reach the terrace Kann first tried the restaurant's rear door, but it was unaccountably locked. And so he made his way back through the restaurant and then through the bar to the front entrance, here wading into a crowd of departing diners who were hurrying to catch the next tram car down the mountain. By the time he arrived at the terrace at the rear of the restaurant Marion was nowhere to be seen. Standing on the spot where he believed he had spied her he noticed that the level stones of the walkway had, it seemed, been recently loosened. Feeling like a fool he nonetheless stood at the edge and, leaning over the railing, called her name. The wind whistled a reply. And then he heard the creaking and groaning of the tram car from the other side of the small wooden bridge. He took one last look round—through the window he could see Walter and Velarde gesticulating at each other with what appeared to be glasses full of dark red wine—and set off at a trot across the awkward walkway, nearly stumbling and going over the side himself as he crossed the bridge.

"Marion?" he called up to the rear side window of the departing tram car. He could not make out her face inside.

"We missed it, too," a man said behind him. "But they run till real late, so never fear."

But Kann did fear as he made his way back to the entrance to the restaurant, as much, he could sense it, for himself as for Marion. Should he check the parking lot where people who drove up the far side of the mountain left their cars? But what if in a fit of rage or pique—but for what reason?—she had hitched a ride down to the city? She'd have left no evidence of her flight. Or what if she were still standing there waiting for a ride? Kann felt the panic rising within him, like the old tides that once must have flooded the great bowl of the high desert valley. She might have left him, he decided, but would she have walked out on an old friend who knew her well enough to speak about her night vision? And what had they done in the dark?

His panic turned to rage, pure jealousy, as he stepped up onto the restaurant steps, determined to take one more look at the place where she—a person—might have fallen, crying out against the air which at ten thousand feet would muffle most any shout. He peered precipitously down at a moonscape shrouded mostly in darkness. And then he straightened his back and turned around, arrested like a deer by the lights flashing from the window behind him. Marion stood there, her face pressed childlike against the glass, holding in her right hand an Indian doll so large and realistically made that it might have been a real, breathing infant suspended miraculously stiff in air. Behind her Walter and Velarde stood grinning, ebullient extras in the comedy of his life. Caught in the act, Kann turned again, this time in shame, and as though it were what he had been intending all along, hauled fluid up from the deepest crevices of his chest and spat into the dark. The wind blew it back in his face.

THE CALL

The woman's voice separated her from the multitudes who communicated each day by means of the great city's telephone system. A deep, wheezing gasp, like the astonished outcry of a dying passenger on a voyage she had begun in good health, it seemed at first hearing to bestow a certain difference, if not distinction, upon my little quest.

"Who are you?"

Not the measured North American "hello" I was accustomed to or the terse, nearly always shouted *Buay-No?* which most natives of the city hurled into the mouthpiece on first picking up the receiver, her words caught me quite by surprise.

I backed up a bit in the mental spaces that separated us, me on the edge of my narrow bed in a dark hotel room in the center of the city, the woman at a location as yet unknown to me—I had a letter with a postal box only as a return address—though somewhere within the boundaries of the city's trunkline.

"Who are you? Do you know who I am?"

My mind flew three thousand miles north and east and then roared back again to the moment's problem. Had I been placing the call from my office I might have been less tense about how to handle the difficulty which seemed to be increasing at each word. One marriage and two children later,

I had put the wreck of myself back together and had an assignment for a story that was going to change more than my life. Like a man favoring an injured limb, I began to speak in a quiet, what I took to be friendly, voice explaining as succinctly as possible the purpose of my call.

"That's not what you want."

Confused for a moment, I lay back on the rough coverlet of my single bed and repeated myself. Despite the temperate climate year round of this city more than a mile above the level of the sea, little sunlight penetrated the cloud cover. Factories to the north coughed out dark smoke, winds pushed the clouds south, mountains behind the city cradled the thickening yellowish air. My room was dim, desolate.

"I know who you are. We met last year."

"I don't think so. I've never been to—"

"You're here! My God, why didn't you say so? Listen, my husband's not home now. Are you downstairs? We can talk."

"I'm in my hotel now. But if you tell me—"

"But you're here. So we can talk. I need to explain to you some of the awful things that have been taking place here. May I tell you truthfully? Forty-five years have gone by without a word of truth. Are you downstairs? My husband will be home soon. We need to prepare ourselves for his arrival. Can we talk?"

"Certainly we can talk. But if you tell—"

"I wouldn't say that if I were you. It's perfectly possible to be truthful downstairs. But up here, I go to my room for such occasions. Didn't you see me leave last year when you came to see my husband? What point of view do you hold?"

"Point of view?" I pretended I didn't understand. But it seemed then the first thing she said that made any sense at all.

"Are you religious?"

"What?"

"Let me write that down. Please, hold the line. I need to find my glasses." Her distinctive breathing faded from the wire, and just below the level of comprehension the twit and chatter of four or five other conversations settled like dust motes on my inner ear. I took out my pencil, doodled in my notebook. I would get my message through and arrange for a rendezvous later in the week. I could pretend with others that my purpose was ordinary, traditional. But a great deal more depended on it than I had cared to admit to anyone but myself.

"Are you political?"

Her voice jarred me into sitting up on the edge of the bed. My pencil fell from my grasp and rolled under the night table.

"Are you downstairs?"

I banged my shoulder retrieving the pencil and suppressed a moan of pain.

"May I give you—"

"Sometimes my husband curses God. He says that God is not listening to us. This, of course, goes to the heart of the system. Forty-five years I have been his companion and now he wants to go traveling with another woman. You're young. I remember you from last year. You have a beard. And didn't I sit quietly in my room? There's no reason for him to do this to me. Excuse me, please, I can't seem to find my glasses. . . ." Again her voice retreated from my ear, only this time not so far away that I could not hear her words melt into terse, hacking sobs.

"Please," I called into the mouthpiece. "Hello. Hello?"

"When you come here you won't see me." Her sobbing ceased abruptly and she was wheezing at me once again. "I will go up to my room. I do my music there. And I have my watercolors and my weaving. If he goes traveling he should take me along. Are you downstairs? I could meet you at the door. Do you promise to speak to me first? I could tell you all you want to know."

"Perhaps you ought to tell me when your husband will be home."

"Never. Or a few minutes. He curses God. Who are you? Your voice is so faint. Are you downstairs?"

"I'm in my hotel. If you tell me when to call back—"

"Are you political? That's an important question. If you tell me that, I will tell you all. Of course, the Jews—"

I cleared my throat.

"You don't know my husband very well, do you?"

"No, I don't."

"But you were here last year. We met downstairs. You had a beard. You were very young."

"Perhaps I ought to call back later, when your husband will be home."

"He doesn't live here anymore."

"He doesn't?"

"Are you downstairs or in your hotel?"

"I am in my hotel. Could you please—"

"Do you want to see my husband today?"

"Yes, I would, if that's—"

"He's dead."

"What? I'm sorry, I'm so sorry."

"Are you religious?"

"I—"

"It doesn't matter. Please wait for me downstairs."

"I'm very sorry."

"Are you political? This has bearing on the question. When my husband comes home, he'll ask these questions. Please understand, I'm writing all of this down. Forty-five years is a long time to be someone's companion. Are you downstairs now? I thought I heard the door."

"I'm very sorry. I didn't know. . . ." I was shaking with confusion. A moment before, I had been hating this sad, crazy woman who stood between me and my goal. Suddenly everything had tilted, all had changed.

"Will you come and watch me pack his bags? I believe we know you from last year. Are you downstairs yet? I am in the room myself. Who are you? Can you help?"

"Is there someone else there I can speak to?"

"Oh, is that what you want after all? Explain to him about the years. Do you promise? If you do, I'll go to my room. I have music there, my weaving."

"I promise. Now please—"

"He just came back now. He went to the dry cleaners. I love you. Why do you ask me that? Here he comes. Years of weaving. Are you political? Do you have the right number? This is a Spanish-speaking household. Please report to the authorities."

She stopped speaking and for a long suspended moment I could hear the sound of furniture scraping across a floor, the tinkle of shattering glass, and behind that the whir and whine of the city's eternal traffic jam from the far side of the telephone line as well as below my window.

"Who is this?"

A man's voice on the wire, the slightest touch of accent, like a daub of dark paint on a blank canvas.

I hurried to explain myself and what I was after.

"How long has my wife been speaking with you?"

I fumbled for a reply.

"I apologize for her behavior. What is it that you want of me?"

I spoke as carefully as I could.

"I'm sorry. I don't give interviews anymore, mister. . . ." He mispronounced my name.

I spoke again, more slowly, trying not to plead.

"I am sorry."

"Your publisher—"

"He doesn't speak for me."

"Your letter—"

"My situation has changed."

"Your work—"

"My work speaks for itself."

"My project—"

"I'm very sorry. Please don't call here again."

Doves congregated on the rooftops, flapping their wings in protest against the metal-heavy air. From dozens of tubs and basins, boisterous water gushed, like sound through wires, setting the walls to trembling with its passage. Surprising me where I lay brooding in my solitude, the maid used her master key to enter my room. She apologized for intruding, bowing her head as she backed out the door. Later, the piercing shriek of rending steel, wailing sirens, voices shrilling in pain and dismay summoned as many of us as could hurry downstairs as witnesses to an accident other than our own.

THE QUEST FOR
AMBROSE BIERCE

1

The bus rolled across the bridge to the south bank of the river and Alman breathed at last. He had imagined it to be a broader, swifter stream, but even so he felt newborn. Dark-faced boys in rags played among weeds and stubby cactus alongside the other shore. They didn't look up as he passed, but he waved anyway.

Oily fumes welled up inside the nearly deserted bus as the vehicle slowed to a crawl and turned into a parking area at the rear of a group of low stone buildings. *Aduana*. Customs. *Immigración*. Immigration. Alman flexed his college Spanish, a legacy that had finally convinced a doubting editor at *Ohio Magazine* to let him give this assignment a try. Inside one of the buildings a small dark man in an unpressed khaki uniform typed up his tourist card. "What for do you take this machine?" he asked, pointing to the small portable typewriter Alman had bought at a Columbus discount store just before he departed. "You are a journalist?" "To write letters home," Alman said with a straight face. The man nodded. "Not do it by hand?" He held up his hand, palm outward, as though showing Alman a secret sign. Alman shook his head. The man grinned and handed him his card. Alman had been warned about stating that he was entering the country in order to write an article. Nobody warned him about the smells, the noise, the sprightly music that rolled out of the loudspeakers in the small food stands on the edge of the parking lot.

"Señor?"

The smiling, round-faced woman touched his arm just as he stepped into the next building for baggage inspection.

He backed away from her, but only far enough to get a good look at her breasts swelling beneath her light synthetic sweater.

"Do you speak English?"

She smiled, as if approving his glance.

"I wan' hep. You give? I be you' mai'?"

"I don't need a maid."

She shook her head.

"Jes' for now, señor. For his 'spectión."

"Oh?" Alman tried to figure out her plan. "You want to say you're my maid when you go through customs?"

"Sí!" She showed him nearly every tooth in her mouth.

They were already walking slowly down the long corridor, their bags in their hands (and a sack slung over the chubby woman's shoulder as well). She didn't look like a drug smuggler or a prostitute. He nodded his agreement. The Mexican woman kept several paces behind him but he could feel her presence. He had a recollection of a news story about Mexican citizens bringing in appliances and new clothes from the U.S. and trying to avoid paying the duty. It was close to Christmas so he figured that this must be the case with the woman who wanted to pose as his maid.

A squat guard patted his typewriter, glanced inside his suitcase, listened to the woman's languid words about her service to this North American. Alman then found himself on the other side of the customs line.

"Gracias," she muttered as they returned to the bus. She placed her bulky sacks in the overhead rack alongside his typewriter and settled into the seat next to him.

He leaned away from her, giving her room to spread her billowy skirt. The woman—she told him her name was Marguerita Aceves after he introduced himself first—settled closer to him. Their thighs met, chaperoned by the folds of her skirt. The bus lurched forward through the desert twilight. Blue-black clouds hovered above distant mountains in the west. The last streaks of sunlight turned muddy beyond them. Joshua trees raised their stubby arms toward the darkening sky. Alman used unhappy memories of the past few lonely months as a sleeping pill. He dozed. Upon awakening, he found Marguerita Aceves's hand lying limply on his thigh. A minute passed in which he enjoyed the touch of her palm just above his kneecap. Then he edged toward the dark aisle. Moments later, her body sagged with the leftward movement of the bus, and her hand flopped back onto his leg, her head against his shoulder.

The bus roared like a dragon, approaching mountains on an endless incline of curves and more curves. It climbed and climbed into the high desert. Marguerita Aceves snored lightly in his ear. He imagined himself in bed with her, on top of her, married to her, raising her children. At least she smuggled for family and not just for herself. A faint tinge of heartburn swelled his chest at the thought of his own marriage in Columbus. But he didn't want to carry such excess baggage with him on this trip. And so he tried to imagine Ambrose Bierce's bitter journey across the desert. And imagined leads for his article, his first but not, he hoped, his last.

Noisily the bus expelled bad gas from its exhaust as it slowed down, steadying into a lower speed, then turning the curve that led westward. Alman must have dozed. Lights of a city flickered across his eyelids. Moments later the bus thumped along a roadway with special strips of concrete spaced out every few yards to slow them down. Alman shook off sleep and gazed at the lights of the bus terminal at the end of the long street.

"Permit me," said the awakening Marguerita, her voice fuzzy with sleep. He launched himself to his feet to allow her to pass down the aisle. As he watched her move lithely toward the door, he felt the heaviness in his bowels, thirst, heavy eyes. A few dark passengers from the rear brushed past him. He plunged after them into the aisle, into the terminal. In the brightly lighted but foul-smelling lavatory, he unloaded his bladder and bowels, then bought a can of papaya juice and returned to the bus. Noxious engine fumes mingled with the flavor of the sweet, thick juice of the tropical fruit.

Old passengers filed back into the vehicle, new ones arrived. A thin woman in black appeared at his side. He shook his head, telling her in signs that the seat was taken. Stoically, she passed on. Next a swarthy Indian peasant. More hand signals. The man protested. Alman sat up to full height. The man shuffled to the rear of the bus. Hurry now, he said to Marguerita Aceves in his mind. She ought to know better. These buses left on schedule. Broom—brooom . . . the driver revved the engine.

He did not panic when the overweight man sat down. Sliding to the window, he searched the terminal yard for a glimpse of Marguerita. The bus bumped over a hump that slowed it before the ticket window at the exit. Foreign chatter exploded around him, then subsided as the passengers settled down for the rest of the ride. No sight of her on the platform, he realized as he twisted around for one final look. He had not asked her her destination. He had not even known what contraband she had been smuggling. She had walked so lightly that it seemed that it must have been small cargo, perhaps even drugs or diamonds. The bus slowly rolled through the outskirts of the city, then plunged into the dark desert again at an ever increasing speed. Alman settled back, closed his eyes, rubbed his nose where the pain still tingled slightly, and tried to rehearse an outline for the article on Bierce. Not until he opened his eyes at the first touch of daybreak, as they slowed down once again amid vast tracts of grey and dun-brown dunes, did he discover that his typewriter was missing.

2

Armed with pen and notebook, Alman continued his search, a little bit wiser about his surroundings. His hotel room in Chihuahua was a perfect base—it was so dust laden and depressing that he hated to return there. This encouraged him to spend hour after hour in the hall of records at the State Capitol, and to take excursions into the countryside where lay small villages frequented by the rebel soldiers of Villa during their campaign here in the north.

North? It was as far south as Alman had ever traveled, and the heat of noon on a winter's day convinced him that he didn't want to travel any further south, even in winter, if he could help it. But this was his story, and if it required that he follow tracks southward he would do so. Besides, he told himself, I might somehow meet up with that woman again and get my typewriter back. And he laughed at himself because he knew how naïve a thought that was.

Much to his own surprise, he accepted the rhythm of his new life in Chihuahua, a round of boring research, spicy meals, churning bowels, and lonely nights. Now and then he ate a new dish that pleased him; from time to time he heard himself making noises resembling laughter and others like cries of pain. No friends, no acquaintances cheered or annoyed him. He avoided calling Columbus although a few afternoons found him straying in the direction of the long-distance office. One morning an old man in the newspaper office showed him a yellowed sheet of newspaper with a story referring to the gringo journalist who was accompanying a Villa scouting expedition on an excursion to the coast. Alman was amused at how dislocated he felt when he left the city in the smelly, fuming third-class bus. He had been there only a week and a half but it had felt like home.

Pez de Espada. The name of his destination made him feel all the more uncertain. It was an ocean name—swordfish—and from his window he saw only desert, hour after hour nothing but flat, sandy plain with a few distant mountains on the horizon. Only after dark did they begin their descent, and though he could not see much more than an occasional light in a peasant hut at the side of the thin highway, he felt the heat of the jungle rising up to meet him even as the bus spiraled its way downward toward the sea. By daybreak they rolled along a track under a canopy of palms and tall bushes, many of them heavy with red and yellow blossoms as large as his fists. The passengers who had boarded with him in Chihuahua trickled away stop by stop in tiny villages nestled along the roadway. Few others boarded. By the middle of the night, Alman had the seat to himself. He had suffered, cramped up in the small space, but he had won some deserved sleep as well.

He awoke to discover the broad curve of the azure Pacific sparkling in the morning light, punishing him with its beauty. As the bus spiraled its way down through the welcoming jungle, he sweated beneath the same blanket that had kept out the chill during the night. Alman stripped it off. The bus rounded a turn in the jungle and a collection of palm-roofed hovels appeared down the road. Beyond them the sea burned with the fire of early morning sunlight. The bus driver spat out an oath.

The bus station was the only modern building in the village—a square stucco structure with posters plastered all over its outside walls and its waiting room laid with dirty tiles on which school children had painted a mural of butterfly-shaped fishing boats putting out to sea. From the ferocious glare of the sun, umbrellas, trees, stucco-roofed and -walled houses offered some surcease. But Alman had little time to worry about the heat.

An infant cried out. He glanced over his shoulder at a short, bulbous-nosed woman bundled up in a serape with an infant bulged against her chest. "Can you help me?"

Her voice was pure New York, so out of keeping with her appearance that Alman first looked around to see if someone else was speaking.

"Hello," he said, finally looking into her eyes. These were brown, as was the fringe of unkempt hair that hung down from beneath the hood formed by her serape. She had large cheeks, pocked and red, and her large nose was also cratered. Either her eyes were her only beautiful feature or they merely looked beautiful by comparison with her face.

"Can you help?"

"What's wrong?" Alman tried to catch a glimpse of the baby that the woman bundled so close to her body. Unlike the silent children he had seen on the streets of Chihuahua, this child made tiny mouselike squeaks that penetrated the heavy cloth in which its mother had swaddled it.

"My name is Marsha." The woman blinked several times. "Tommy Alman."

"Tommy," she said, as though she had known him since grade school, "I need your help."

"What's wrong?" He swung his hand around and touched his wallet, an action that had become a habit since his encounter with Marguerita Aceves. Then he felt silly to imagine that he might be threatened by this dumpy American girl with her pathetic bundle.

"Help me get the bus to the border, I'm afraid to go by myself."

The woman trembled, and the cloth fell away from her head, revealing a tangled mess of dirty orange hair that was dark at the roots. She smiled feebly, yet invitingly, motioning toward the baby clothes heaped at her feet.

Alman paused a moment, as if thinking it over, but he was not truly thinking. In Columbus he had returned early from a trip to New York and had walked into his living room to find his wife in the arms of a stranger, and he walked out again, bumping his nose and shoulder against the door frame as he departed, returning to the office to demand an assignment and receiving the word about Bierce. Alman now picked up the bundle and headed to the ticket window.

3

He had made a number of stupid mistakes in his life, but they seemed nothing compared to the troubles of Marsha Meinrich, or Em, as she said her friends called her at college.

"I was an English major," she said, "but really I was into Latin-American stuff. Have you read . . . ?" She named some authors whose names Alman didn't recognize. But then he had never read much; he had, in fact, never read Bierce until he had left the magazine office and stopped at a bookstore, found a couple of his books and then decided to take the bus south so that he had time to study them. He wanted to mention his assignment (or what *had* been his assignment; he had to admit to himself now that the bus took a curve that cut them off at last from the sight of the sea), but Marsha kept on chattering.

"Teatro Boriqueño. Ever hear of that?"

"Sorry. What was that?"

"You weren't listening, Tommy. I said I met Enrique at the Teatro Boriqueño. The Puerto Rican Street Theater where I was an intern over the summer? He was one of the directors. He never went past eighth grade, but he read a lot of drama on his own and wrote some wild plays and also directed them. We were very simpatico, and I moved in with him on the Lower East Side. We had a really grungy place over on East 2nd Street, the part that looks like East Berlin, but we loved each other and it didn't matter. Enrique was getting back to his roots, so I had to learn Spanish, which was really neat, because even though I was away from him during the spring term, I felt close to him during the week because of my Spanish class; anyway it turned out I was pregnant and one of his things was his macho pride so that he didn't want me to get an abortion even though my parents were going crazy, and so I moved in with him at the end of the term. His family wanted us to get married, my family wanted an abortion, and I didn't know what I wanted except Enrique, so we got a little money together from friends and selling things and moved down here, not to Pez but to Oaxaca and then over here to Pez; the baby was born in Oaxaca and then Enrique decided he had to make some money and. . . ."

They traveled for several hours while she put the story together for him, and he was as interested in the news about herself that she was giving him as in the terrain he had missed in the dark.

". . . you know they bust you here for the smallest amount of anything, I mean, like aspirin without a prescription makes them look cross-eyed at you; it's a racket they use to shake down gringos, and I begged and begged him to stop carrying the stuff but he didn't listen, and one day he was up in the city and bam! They picked him up and locked him in and except for a visit a couple a months ago, I haven't seen him. . . ."

What an idiot that Enrique was! Alman wanted to tell her. But since it had taken her so long to get control of herself in order to tell him her story, he feared upsetting the balance she had regained. She had been through a lot of bad times and didn't need him to chip away at her feelings. If for no other reason than taking care of the baby, he didn't want her to become hysterical. Her plan was to cross back over into the States, call her parents, and then find a lawyer for Enrique. But what was his story? The bus rocked from side to side on the narrow highway through the jungle as he gave her an account of his own. Their hips bumped together and he told his tale in bits and pieces, wondering now and then about the lust he felt rising in his lap since she was such a striking picture of ugliness.

She wanted to stop in Chihuahua to buy some supplies for the baby.

"It's been weeks," she said, her voice returned to what was obviously its full strength, "since this little kitten has had clean diapers."

In the cool shade of the drugstore, Alman volunteered to pay for the box of paper diapers.

"Kleen-Bebé," she read from the label, "far out." Then she thrust the infant into his arms and announced that she was going shopping. "I'll meet you back at the bus station."

"What time?" he called after her, the unfamiliar bundle squirming in his arms.

"When does the bus leave?" she asked over her shoulder.

He told her the time.

"I don't know anything about what to do with this!"

"It's good practice!" she said, waddling off along the sun-bleached avenue, leaving him the object of curiosity of a number of admiring pedestrians. The infant had calmed down, but now he realized that it was giving off a sweetish but repugnant odor. Wandering back toward the bus station, he spied a small park and lay the baby down on the grass, letting it kick and make fists at the trees. He undid its filthy wrapping, marveling that a few thin streaks of matter could emit such a foul smell. He daubed carefully at the boy's genitals with his handkerchief—which he then rolled up into a ball and left lying at the base of a tree—and after ruining the tape on only two diapers, successfully negotiated the change.

Vendors approached him, asking him to buy slices of fruit or vegetables, roasted seeds and nuts. He didn't feel hungry although he hadn't eaten in half a day. When the infant stopped its silent calisthenics and slept, he dozed off, only to be awakened by a pinch on his neck and another on his cheek. A scouting party of red ants had attacked him, and as he brushed them aside, he remembered the baby. But the thing slept peacefully, apparently invulnerable to the marauding insects.

"Hey!"

Alman looked up to see Marsha kicking the grass in front of him with the toe of a cowboy boot. She wore a western shirt, faded jeans, and her hair was pulled back to show off all the more starkly the jutting ugliness of her nose and the craters of cheeks. But now that she had shed her serape, he could see a nicely shaped body that distracted him from the unpleasantness of her face.

"Where'd you change?" Alman asked, sitting up and then scooping up the baby into his arms.

Marsha smiled. "You look good with the kid, man. I met a friend of Enrique's. He let me clean up in his place."

"You should have taken the baby with you," Alman said. "It smells."

Marsha relieved him of the child.

"Can't face up to the essential odor of the human race, can you, man? I thought we were supposed to meet in the bus station. I was looking all over for you."

"You didn't think I'd run off with him, did you?"

He stood up and they started walking toward the station, Alman slinging her bags over his shoulders, Marsha with the baby in her arms.

"Actually I think you'd be very good with it." She smiled slyly.

Alman thought she was taunting him and ignored her look. They had missed one bus to the border and now had an hour to wait for another. While Marsha sat on a bench and opened her blouse to nurse the baby, he went out to buy them some food for the trip.

Darkness settled over the desert by the time they rolled north out of the flat, dry city. El Paso, their destination, lay hours away across the dunes. Marsha, in the window seat, asked him to hold the baby while she ate, and then did the same for him. The food was peppery, but the milk nicely cooled his burning tongue.

"He'll sleep all the way," Marsha said, "and I'll change him just before we cross the border so that he doesn't make a mess while we're in customs. Like I once got stuck there for hours one time with Enrique, man, and the baby nearly went berserk."

"Is that where he got caught?"

"Huh? Oh, yeah, but not at the border. He was driving along in Sinaloa and ran into a roadblock. What a bad break, man. They wanted to crucify him and now he's rusting away in prison." There was something in her voice that disturbed him.

"I hope you're going to try and do something for him once you get home."

Marsha had been bumping shoulders with him as they rode. Now she pulled herself toward the window.

"What kind of a chick do you think I am?"

Alman retreated as far as he could toward the aisle.

"I don't know, Marsha, it just sounded like—"

"Let me tell you, everything isn't always the way it sounds. And that's not something they teach you real well in college. Tommy, you think it's time to get aggressive with me? Now I know exactly why your wife left you."

The remark hit Alman in the chest like a fist.

"Why was that?"

"Because you pretend you're macho when you're really just a pushover."

Marsha burped loudly, adjusted the sleeping baby in the crook of her arm as though the infant were a limp-limbed rag doll, closed her eyes, and went to sleep.

A large, bright moon dominated the desert highway. Alman would have liked to have blamed its piercing light for his own inability to sleep, but he knew that what kept him awake were the facts of his life rolling about in his brain like loose luggage on the upper rack of the bus. Without even feeling very sorry for himself, he understood that up until now his days had simply caved in on him, like sand in a pit in the desert through which the bus now carried him.

Though he was rolling north toward the border of his country and knew absolutely nothing about what he would do once he got there, he prayed that he would find something. Something. Something. To the tune of his seatmate's stertorous breathing, finally he dozed.

More than a moment but less than an hour had gone by when he opened his eyes. The moon had slipped down behind them, and the bus roared forward toward Texas and darkness. Either the baby or the woman had stirred, rousing him from his slumber. When he moved slightly in the seat, he felt the heel of a hand resting on his upper thigh while the fingers worked open the zipper of his corduroy trousers.

He glanced over at Marsha, but she lay back, eyes closed, the baby still asleep on her arm, as though she knew nothing about the stealthy, steady progress of her own hand. Suddenly she had the zipper unlatched, and spread open the metal teeth. Like a ferret after a rabbit, her hand swiftly entered the slit in the front of his undershorts and grasped his flaccid penis.

The shock pressed him back against the seat, and he rolled his eyes about, fearing that some full-bladdered passenger might this very moment stumble down the aisle toward the bathroom in the rear of the bus. But no one stirred; only the fuss and roar of the engine, and the thud of the tires on the bumpy desert highway, broke the silence that encircled him like her fingers tightening around his organ. It was a dream, it was a fantasy out of the pages of a magazine, it was a dilemma, it was a pleasure, it was a tricky quickening sense of the improbable taking place right there in his own lap, a daydream at night, a surging, mounting, thickening, a blurring of sight and urging of feeling, a bucking of his hips; he spurted into her hand.

No less quickly than she had found him, she pulled away, sliding her slick fingers across his thighs. She wiped them on the baby's blanket, and withdrew back into the sleep that she had surprised him from, like a sea animal retiring into its shell. Alman, lulled into a stupor, closed his eyes, listened to the bus, remembering only when he noticed the shape of another passenger against the darkness of the aisle that he had to adjust his trousers.

He must have slept because a faint touch of light dappled the horizon just beyond the supine girl's shoulder. He was glad that she hadn't awakened because it gave him a minute to decide how to treat the whole thing when she opened her eyes. As it turned out, he needed no strategy. When in the next few moments the bus swerved to avoid a cow grazing at the roadside, Marsha sat up, bright-eyed, and inquired after the time. When he told her, she beamed.

"We're almost to the border," she said. "Don't you need to take a piss or something? I want to stretch out and change the baby."

He nodded, pleased that nothing of their encounter in the darkness showed in her eyes. He got up, and she immediately set down the sleeping infant in his seat, reaching into her knapsack for a fresh diaper. The stench inside the tiny bathroom nearly made him gag. But he took advantage of the small sink with the pump faucet to wash himself. When he returned to the middle of the bus, Marsha was nursing the baby, whose tiny, birdlike noises spoke of hunger unlike any he had known in a long while.

The moon had departed; the sun lolled up over the dunes. Within minutes he could make out the towers and rooftops of Juarez with El Paso on the northern bank of the winking river. In a few more minutes, they were rolling past shacks made of corrugated tin, and then small brick houses with dry front yards full of cactus trees and bluebonnets. They had to switch buses at the Juarez station for their trip across the border. With its odor of insecticide, whiskey, cigarettes, and body odor, the ancient vehicle that carried them onto the bridge might have been the same one that had transported him southward only a few weeks ago. Except that this time no dumpy Mexican woman looked nervously about as they approached the customs checkpoint. Only a few laborers who had boarded in Juarez accompanied him and Marsha into the U.S. customs building at the side of the broad cement bridgeway.

A dour Mexican official collected their tourist cards— and then motioned for them to move on to American territory. There a uniformed Texan, narrow as a reed, looked him in the eye, asking if they had anything to declare.

"No, sir," Alman said.

"Open these, please," the official said stiffly, rummaging through Alman's small suitcase and Marsha's knapsack.

"How old's the baby?" he asked.

Alman said, "Uh . . ."

"New fathers!" Marsha broke in with a snort, telling the man the infant's age in months.

The man kept on feeling about in the knapsack, but his voice took on a more gentle quality than the movement of his hand suggested.

"That all you have with you, son?"

Alman nodded.

"I had a typewriter but it was stolen."

"That's the way it is down there," the official said, as though he were talking about a pit or the ocean bottom. "Okay, you can get back on the bus now."

"Thank you, sir," Alman said. Marsha remained silent as they left the customs booth and reboarded the reeking bus. When they were turning down a short street that led to the El Paso Greyhound Station, she said, quietly, "You're terrific."

Alman had no idea what she meant, and was still too embarrassed about the incident in the night to ask about it. At least one thing had become clear: he wasn't going back to work for the magazine, and that was fine with him.

"Baby needs a change," Marsha declared when the bus came to a stop.

"I'll do it," Alman volunteered, pulling their luggage down from the rack and following her out of the bus and into the depot. They had a number of benches to choose among in the nearly deserted station. Marsha selected one in the corner by the baggage room which at this hour had not yet opened. She spread a blanket on the bench and gently lay the infant on top of it.

"Listen, you check the time of the New York bus, okay, honey? I'll change the baby."

"Honey?" Alman saw that she was about to pull open the baby's diaper. "Okay." He ambled over toward the ticket counter where the schedule was mounted on a board in white plastic letters and numbers. New York? Why New York? Her husband was in jail in Mexico. Why did she want to go all the way up to New York? Maybe he could convince her to go somewhere else. She seemed quite footloose for all of the needs of the baby. He checked the time of the next bus to New York but also of the next one to Los Angeles. He'd only been there a few times selling space, but it was a new town and maybe a better town for him, or them, than New York.

"I'm just going to get rid of this poo-poo," Marsha said when he returned to the bench. She held up at arm's length a neatly folded diaper.

Alman nodded, sitting down alongside the infant who seemed to be asleep again and watching Marsha walk slowly off in search of a place to dispose of the loaded diaper.

She folds a diaper nice, he thought, deciding that he would attempt to talk her out of going to New York and into trying another town, maybe L.A. or Houston; he had sold space in Houston, too, and it was a growing town. You don't want to go all that far away from your husband, do you? he'd say. Think of the baby, he'll want to see the baby. I'll convince her. She probably only wants to go to see her own family a while and then come back down. He remembered what she did for him in the dark of the bus. We'll stop, we'll take a hotel room. He pictured all kinds of pleasure for them in the dark room.

A bus full of workers from the other side of the river unloaded noisily, filling the depot with Spanish and cigarette smoke. Alman stood up and looked around. She's in the ladies, he decided.

A second busload of workers arrived. The ticket seller opened the booth, illuminating his sign with a flick of a switch. Alman poked around in the knapsack, found that it was full of paper diapers and small bottles, cans of powdered milk, clothing. A policeman appeared in the center of the depot, and when he strolled near the bench, Alman, for some reason he could not explain, turned to look after the baby.

The ticket seller called out the times of departing buses. When Alman heard the New York bus announced he picked up the sleeping infant, amazed as before at its near weight-lessness, and hurried outside into the light of full dawn. Marsha wasn't anywhere in sight. He rushed back to check the gate where a small group of dark-skinned travelers shuffled in toward the bus.

"New York?" asked the driver at the gate.

Alman shook his head, retreating to the bench.

"Jesus," he muttered. He waited on the bench a while longer, then scooped up child, knapsack, and his own suit-case, and walked to the ticket counter. "Did you see?" The baby stirred, and he rocked it gently in his arms, hoping that it would remain asleep.

"Is it boy?" The brown-skinned ticket seller looked at him blankly.

Alman nodded.

"What's it call?"

Alman shook his head.

Later, as they departed for Las Cruces, with the morning sun behind them, Alman, hands trembling, heart beating wildly despite the calm and certitude of the humming American bus, patted the wailing infant on its bottom until its noisy fears subsided. In Tucson, amidst the ammoniac fumes of the men's room, he changed the infant yet one more time. In Phoenix, after picking a cigarette butt from the drain, he sat the naked creature in the sink, bathed it with a paper towel and rubbed it with ointment he found in the knapsack. Dabbing water on its brow, he took a deep breath and gave the child an old-fashioned masculine name.

ACCIDENT

As though someone had stalked up behind him and given a forceful, two-handed shove, Joseph French, a TVA engineer, stumbled across the threshold of the day-care center, managing somehow to keep a small boy aloft in his arms.

"Damn!" he said, surprising himself with the sound of his own voice. It had been months since he had let himself speak out with such feeling.

"I told you," said a frizzy-haired blonde girl in her early twenties, dressed in faded jeans and a Smoky Mountain T-shirt that fitted snugly across her chest. She was looking at French but talking to a moon-faced older woman in a red pantsuit who, in turn, was staring at him.

"Good morning," the older woman said with a drawl. "I'm Mrs. McEnry, and this is Sue Gail Mabry, one of our regular teachers. Except today she's making to leave for the courthouse to get rid of a husband who's been giving her a bucketful of troubles."

"This is Billy," the engineer said. He found himself staring into the cornflower blue eyes of the Mabry girl. The room smelled of disinfectant and crayons. None of the other children seemed to have arrived.

"I been telling her to fix that carpet for weeks now," the girl said, flashing him a quick smile. "We got to fix it before somebody has a real bad accident." She reached over and gave the child a pat on the nose. Billy began to shriek.

"Aw, I just can't do nothing right," Sue Gail said. "I better go and say my part. Bye, you all." She made a little mock curtsy, and hurried out the door.

Billy had stopped crying by the time the engineer went out the door to his car. The young father drove along the tree-lined hilly road in the direction of town. It was his first day on the job and this brought a lot of worries. Nonetheless, he felt reassured by Mrs. McEnry's manner and hopeful that Billy would have a good place to stay. He deserved one.

"Damn!" the engineer said, raising a fist and pounding it against the steering wheel. "Damn!"

He could see clouds as he drove; he could see the ghostly shapes of the mountains rising out of the hazy east. There were huge constructions out there he had been hired to maintain. Water rose, locks clicked, fields of transformers hummed and buzzed beneath towering shields of concrete and steel. His life on the other hand was a mournful mess, shards of metal on a highway, blood, bone, an empty place at the table, a narrow bed.

Billy was alert and babbling when, at six that evening, Mrs. McEnry handed him back. She delivered a verbal report on the child's day: his naps and eating habits, his bowel movements (there was some question of trouble here) and his several moods. The engineer listened as carefully as he would if he had been subject to a report on the qualities of a new method of pouring stone. The room gave off the odor of milk and skin and feces. Half a dozen children still remained here at the end of the day, some listless, some animated, all of them gravitating slowly toward his legs, toward the door.

"That other teacher come back?" he heard himself ask as he adjusted his squirming child in his arms. He looked about at the walls papered with smeary finger paintings and collages made of pine twig and milk carton, which his son was still far too young to construct. His feet ached, though he had sat all day at his new desk. His chest felt hollow, like the model of a chest.

"Sue Gail? She come back for a little while and then she went home. It's a hard thing."

"It's not easy," he said, looking down at the torn carpet. "What I told you over the phone about?"

"Yes," she said in a voice soft enough to be reserved for children only.

"Well, good night," he said, stepping carefully back over the threshold. "See you tomorrow."

It was nearly nine o'clock before the engineer, his shirt stained with milk and spittle, his back aching from his labor, tiptoed from the room of his sleeping child and fixed himself a drink. A sheaf of reports as thick as an eastern Sunday newspaper waited for him in his briefcase, but he found himself standing at the sink of the kitchenette in his new two-bedroom apartment when the telephone rang.

"Quiet!" he said aloud. Scotch splashed on his hands and shirt-sleeves as he slapped down his glass and lunged for the phone.

"Hello?"

"Mr. French?"

"This is Joe French. Who's calling?"

"This is Sue Gail Mabry, from the day-care center? Except I'm not at the day-care center right now, I'm down at Buddy's Barbecue?"

"Yes?"

"I hope I'm not bothering you too late?"

"No, you're not bothering me."

"Well, now, Mr. French, I'm calling to tell you how sorry I was about upsetting little Benny."

"Billy," he corrected her.

"That's right, Billy, because it wasn't till later that Mrs. McEnry explained everything to me, about your wife and the accident. And it got me thinking, what with spending a day in court divorcing and all, I just wanted to call and tell you I was sorry."

"Well, Sue Gail," French said, "Mrs. McEnry told me about your going to court and I understand how you could be upset, so don't let it bother you."

"Mr. French, I just didn't want to be responsible for making any more trouble for that little boy."

French recalled vividly the weeping and wailing of that evening's bedtime. But he said, merely, "He's fine, he's been through a lot but just doesn't know much about it, lucky kid, he's too young."

There was a pause at the other end of the line during which the engineer thought he heard music, laughing voices, shouts. When he held the telephone away from his ear for a moment, the silence of his apartment and the building was overwhelming by comparison.

"Ever have any of this good barbecue?" the girl was saying when he touched the receiver to his ear again.

"Did I ever? Sure, I'm sure I must have."

"Bet you never tasted this stuff down here at Buddy's."

French found himself shaking his head and backing up to the counter where he placed his drink. "I just moved here."

"Then you just sit tight."

"What do you mean?"

"You just sit tight because I'm going to deliver you some of this barbecue!"

When fifteen minutes later the bell rang, the engineer rose leadenly and dragged himself across the room, convinced that he was condemning himself to whatever happened next because he didn't want the bell to wake Billy. As he turned the knob and pulled the door inward, he had a terrible thought: he wished that he had also died in the crash.

"Surprise!"

The girl from the day-care center, wearing the same clothes as when they first met, stood in the doorway with a paper sack in one hand and a six-pack of bottled beer in the other.

"You don't latch your door," she said, forcing him to make way for her as she crossed the threshold. "That's a dangerous way to live around these parts. Somebody could rob you or give you real trouble."

French shut the door behind them but deliberately did not slip on the latch. There was an air about her that he had not noticed on their first meeting, a certain sense of disruption or danger, so that he quite unaccountably felt the fear rise in him. But when she crossed the room he considered that he must be mistaken because no woman with so slim a body, such narrow hips, slight breasts and tiny ankles, could ever be a threat. Except one way, he reminded himself, following her across the room in the wake of the fierce odor of barbecue.

"Where's your picnic table, buddy?" she inquired as though she were nothing but a delivery girl.

"Straight ahead," French said, directing her to the kitchen.

"Nice place," she said after setting down the sack and the beer on the counter. "Real modern. I been living with Eddie in a trailer for two years now out on the Clinton Highway? He always promised me a place like this, but never come through." She worked a beer out of the cardboard container and handed a bottle to him and then took another for herself. "Eddie's been my ex all of half a day, but I hope never to see him again. 'Cept I have." Her voice trailed off as she fiddled with her beer.

"He still around?"

"Around, upside down and all over the place, like cow flop." She gasped as the top of her beer bottle popped off in her fingers. "I'm telling you, Mr. French, these boys around here are spoiled by their mamas into thinking they're the greatest and spoiled by their papas into thinking they're the toughest. It don't do no one no good in the outcome." She raised her bottle toward him. "You got a special way of saying?"

French looked at his bottle, still capped, and worked the top loose.

"My wife and I used to say, 'cheers.' I don't know where we picked that up. Neither of us have—had—ever been to England."

He raised the bottle, clanked it lightly against hers, drew it to his lips and drank.

"Cheers," the girl said.

"Cheers," he repeated after a few swallows. "I suppose we ought to eat that food. How much was it? I'll pay you back."

"It's your money already," Sue Gail said, leaning back against the sink. Another girl he might have thought was showing off her chest for him but French told himself that Sue Gail Mabry was merely making herself at home.

He took another swallow from the bottle, hoping that on top of everything else he had drunk the beer might calm him. But it had the opposite effect.

"Mine? How?" he asked, madly tapping his foot.

"You pay for day-care, don't you? Or you will be. And they pay me."

"Got you," French said, relaxing a bit. He had been waiting for something more complicated if not profound, and he was pleased when her answer was so simple.

"That farm boy Eddie sure didn't like me working there. Or anywhere. He was so backward! He said 'a woman's place is you-know-where.' Shoot, that stuff used to work back in the dark ages, but it sure don't mean much today. Now your wife worked, didn't she?"

French nodded. "She was a government typist."

Sue Gail opened her mouth wide.

"Secret documents and all?"

"Reports on dam inspections. I'm part of a dam-inspecting team."

Sue Gail's eyes lighted up.

"You're one of those damn inspectors!"

"I've only heard that joke five thousand times. But you make it sound funny even so."

"I'm a funny girl, Mr. French. Everyone I know comments on my good sense of humor. Down at day-care I sure do try to keep the girls laughing. Only one whose funnybone I never could tickle was that damn Eddie, if you pardon my language." She sucked long and hard from her bottle. "Margie, Mrs. McEnry, she told me on the phone what an idiot I was. I really am sorry about your wife, Mr. French; I'm sorry I made that little boy—"

"Please call me Joe," he said, standing up and going to the door. At first he had thought it was Billy who had either fallen out of his crib or thumped it against the bedroom wall. But now he ascertained that a sound was coming from the hallway, possibly on the landing below.

"Mr. French," the girl asked, "how many of these buildings are there in this apartment place?"

"In the complex? Three."

"Lordy."

They were both standing at the door now, their food and drink back on the kitchen counter.

"What's wrong?"

"I parked all the way over on the far building, thinking he wouldn't look in this one."

A shout echoed in the hall.

"That's Eddie," Sue Gail said. "I'll tend to him. He's just feeling sorry for himself."

"He followed you from the barbecue place?"

Sue Gail nodded as she opened the door.

"Come on down here, stupid!" she called. "The judge told you not to follow me!"

She was about to step into the hall when French reached for her arm.

"Don't."

It was the first time that he stood this close to her and he could smell the odor of cigarettes on her hair, as well as the beer and barbecue on her breath, her sweat and the faintest touch of some kind of herbal perfume shampoo. Fine dark hairs cloaked her lower arm, and as she turned toward him he felt her muscles surge beneath his fingers.

"You're a nice man. He was chasing me and I had nowhere else to hide." She broke his grip. "I'm sorry."

"Invite him in," French said, amazed at his own voice.

"You sure? Won't take but a few minutes to calm him down, and this way he won't wake up the whole building."

"That's what I was thinking. Just as long as he . . ."

"Long as he what?" asked the slightly built, dark-haired man wearing a pepper-and-salt beard as he pushed against the door.

"As long as he won't wake this man's little boy baby, that's what."

Sue Gail took the intruder by the arm.

"Eddie, you're drunk, and disobeying a court order."

"That ain't all I'm going to disobey," Eddie said, pulling the door closed behind him. He withdrew a small blue-steel revolver from his coverall pocket. French stepped back across the room.

"This your new man?"

He gestured with the gun. French tried to keep himself from flinching but couldn't.

"You know I ain't got nobody new. I just don't want nobody old."

"Cute, ain't she?" As the man addressed French, he lowered the weapon a degree or two.

"I d-don't know," French said.

"You got a little boy?"

French nodded.

Sue Gail made a noise of disgust.

"He just put him to bed and you're going to wake him by behaving younger than he is."

Eddie ignored her.

"I got a boy, seven, lives with his grandmother in Sunbright."

Once again French found himself looking at Sue Gail.

"I'm not the mother of that child, if that's what you're thinking," she said. "That child's by the *first* woman dumb enough to marry him."

"Shut up now," Eddie said. "She sure don't like me, does she?" he said to French. "Now you might ask how I went and married somebody don't like me as much as she don't. And I can't answer that, because she liked me well enough at first. And now she don't like me much at all. She got a whole lot of feelings for strangers' kids over at that center, but she don't have one ounce of care for me."

"That's because you act about two years old. No woman wants a man acts two years old." Sue Gail for the first time let her eyes linger on the gun. "Let's go out of here and talk."

"Sure, we'll talk, just like old times, talking, talking. But my gut is busting. Mister, you got a . . . ?"

"Sure," French said, trying to be as agreeable as possible. "Down the hall and first door on the left."

Eddie flashed him a quick smile.

"Appreciate it."

Stuffing the gun into his belt, he walked lithely past them into the hall.

"Don't you be long," Sue Gail called after him. "Mr. French, I'm awfully sorry, but he was following me all around the barbecue place, and I knew I couldn't go back to Margie McEnry's. She's just had a bellyful of Eddie and me, so I called her and got your number and address. It's a sorry thing, but believe it or not I just had nobody else would put up with me anymore. I got a sister, but she lives over near Cherokee." Her voice turned soft and childlike. "Both my folks is dead."

Now that Eddie had left the room, French calmed down long enough to breathe.

"I understand."

At least he thought that he did. He was wondering what he could say to her next when he heard the distant murmur of the toilet flushing and the sound of someone clearing his throat.

"Maybe . . . ," he began, but Sue Gail touched a finger to his lips.

French felt his head pounding. There was something about her touch, her presence, that both confused him and made him wonder; it drew him in.

Then came the explosion from the hallway. At first he thought it was the plumbing, or somehow, ridiculously, the telephone, or the ceiling, or a car in the parking lot backfiring, or a TV imploding, a balloon bursting, or his heart thumping louder than his life. By the time he turned his leaden body around, Sue Gail had raced past him. She scarcely stopped for a second at the entrance to the bathroom, peeking in as though on a neighbor whose door she had mistakenly opened, and then hurrying toward the bedroom as though she had always known the way.

French paused much longer than she did at the doorway, assailed by the bitter stench of gunpowder, urine and his own fierce sweat like razors at his nose. As though setting a stage in a high school play, someone had splashed blood across the wall behind the fixtures and barred the door from opening any further with a prop or a booted foot. After what felt like wading through waters rising in a dream, he reached Billy's cribside. Sue Gail already held him in her arms, crooning to him in her sweet, twangy voice, "There, there . . . there, there." The child was silent. But as French's eyes grew accustomed to the dark, he saw his son was wide-awake and smiling.

"He had a 'accident,' " Sue Gail said, "but it's all right, it's all right."

TOWARD EASTER ISLAND

At the counter the attendant told him the news.

She was a plump woman with cocoa-hued cheeks and forehead. Her lips were painted red ochre, the color of cave paintings he had seen in France and Asia. Her accent revealed the slightest trace of a foreign language. He was the one flying, but she seemed nervous. Her hand fluttered about her face, like a bird that refused out of fear to alight. A wedding band flashed mischievously before his eyes.

"I guess we wait a while," Bunch said, more to himself than anyone else since the attendant had already turned toward the next passenger in line. He walked into the waiting room and looked out through the wall-length window. Sure enough, their luggage bumped down the conveyer belt from the large silver plane parked at the gate.

"They've got explosive-sniffing dogs," said a voice at his ear. A bearded man about ten years Bunch's junior stood next to him at the window, shuffling his feet and rubbing his hands together as though he were in the Arctic rather than the Miami airport.

Bunch, usually a friendlier person, merely nodded. He was wondering if Mira had called it in.

"German shepherds," the bearded man said. "I read about it in the papers, man. The police department keeps half a dozen of the suckers just for times like this."

Bunch momentarily wondered about the man, his dark beard, his long, quite delicate eyelashes, his pale blue eyes. His clothing appeared to be that of a graduate student or a rich boy on a lark. Or was he a smuggler taking a round-about route to cocaine country? Standing in the men's room, staring at his face in the mirror alongside the wall where someone had scrawled in lipstick "Cubans Go Home," he pictured Miriam Cohen Bunch telling her story into his beard. He could hear her voice at least as clearly as those crackling out of the loudspeaker announcing arrivals, departures, delays.

Lightning sparked at a distance as they bounded the gulf, and it tracked them as they crossed the cordillera, as though the gods were retreating south toward the pole under heavy mortar attack. Had there been a passenger in the seat next to him, Bunch might have remarked about the bomb threat. As it was, he had to keep his worries to himself, only now and then allowing the question to come to the surface— between the hot face towels and wine and food passed out by the stiff, trim, pale-skinned stewardesses whose French sometimes overpowered their English in announcements from the front of the airplane. But when the wheels touched down, he remembered that he had forgotten about the bomb for nearly the last third of the flight.

"Man goin' 'round takin' names."

The bearded passenger moved up behind him in the line that led to the kiosk where a dour official in blue uniform and cap sat hunched over a sheaf of documents.

"That's the List, man," he said. "I'll bet they check up on me just 'cause of the way I look."

When it was his turn, Bunch stepped up to the kiosk and had a good look at the thick, bound computer print-out through which the official had been thumbing. The man motioned for Bunch to hand over his passport.

"Is he checking you out?" the bearded man said from behind.

Bunch shrugged. The official had already closed the book and slid his passport back across the counter.

"Mr. Bunch?"

A round-faced man in a brown crewneck sweater and baggy corduroys was waiting for him on the other side of the gate from Immigration.

"Yamaguchi," he said, offering his hand. "Public Affairs Officer. I've got a driver waiting outside." Bunch was sitting in the rear passenger seat of the Chevy van watching the door of the airport when he saw the bearded fellow emerge from the entrance with two uniformed men at either side. Then the driver came around and blocked his view.

"It's a little chilly here, isn't it?" Yamaguchi said from the front seat, laughing at his own joke. "You came out of spring. This is our autumn."

"I feel it," said Bunch.

"How was your flight?"

"Aside from the bomb threat? Just fine."

"Well," said Yamaguchi, "you can rest up, take a tour of the city, get briefed. Your flight out doesn't leave until Tuesday."

Bunch leaned forward as the van started up and watched his face in the rearview mirror.

They drove him to a large stone building that occupied nearly an entire block on one of the main squares.

"The Moneda's over there," Yamaguchi said, gesturing toward the dimly lighted far side of the square, but Bunch missed the reference.

It was quite late. The lobby was quiet. He followed the bell captain up the smoothly polished stone stairs to the reception desk on the second floor.

There was a wire waiting for him at the desk.

UCKFAY OUYAY I'M STAYING WITH HIM

A few bellhops murmured in Spanish. The elevator purred open its doors. Out stepped a man wearing a green velvet suit with spangles glittering at his shoulders. Inside the elevator a sign announced the floor show at the poolside bar. On Bunch's floor a tall, husky plainclothesman looked up from his newspaper and nodded to the new arrival. Bunch locked the door to the room behind him and went immediately to the bathroom. He stared at his face in the mirror.

"Ron?"

Bunch looked up from his eggs and toast. The cafeteria on the ground floor was crowded but quiet, and the voice of the man who hailed him sounded like a shot fired over the heads of the other diners.

"I thought you'd be here," Bunch said to the slick-haired, red-cheeked man advancing toward his table.

"What do you mean thought? I'm listed on the program right along with you." He tapped the back of the chair opposite Bunch. "Do you mind?"

Bunch shook his head.

"I didn't see any program."

"You just haven't looked then. Say, aren't you feeling well? You look like hell."

"Long tiring flight. We had a bomb threat. Had to wait in Miami for hours until they got us another plane."

"You look as though you are a walking bomb threat, old boy. Don't tell me—troubles again with the little lady?"

Bunch set down the fork.

"She didn't want me to come."

"Violates her principles, does it? Well, it would be quite pleasant to stay at home and dream up all our stuff. Save us a lot of wear and tear—and bomb threats. But, unfortunately, it's not like that, is it?"

"She doesn't understand science," Bunch said, looking down at his plate.

"Neither do I. But I respect it. Christ, if you were an M.D. would she get angry if you treated a wounded Ku Klux Klansman or such?"

"Not if she had wounded him," Bunch said, feeling his face crack in a smile.

He had several hours before his scheduled briefing and so he set out on a walk. He had a small city map supplied by the embassy and a number of landmarks which Mira had impressed upon him during their arguments. The Moneda Palace was first. It was only a few hundred yards from the entrance to the hotel and appeared to be made of the same stone. All its windows were boarded. Above the main entrance, bullets and mortars had chipped away at the old, dark façade. A sign declared that restoration was in progress under the direction of a local architect.

Nothing seemed out of the ordinary on the Alameda. Thousands of shopkeepers, shoppers, and businessmen crowded the sidewalk. He watched. He waited. Whatever troubles had migrated here had gone underground. While climbing the steep, chipped steps to the top of the Santa Lucia hill, he smelled urine in the corners of the upper terrace; the air was so clear the odors seemed sharper than at home.

"Can't beat this view, can you?"

Bunch, leaning on the stone railing on the uppermost terrace of the hill, had been admiring the snow-smeared Andes, which formed three-quarters of a giant wall around the city. The presence of the bearded man reminded him of the flight, the bomb threat. The first time he saw him, the fellow had only vaguely resembled Arn Jennings—now it was as if the man had had plastic alterations performed on his face during the night.

"You're not a graduate student, are you?" Bunch asked.

The bearded boy laughed. "Are you kidding?"

"Sorry—you look a little like a graduate student I once taught."

"With this beard I look like a lot of people, man. But I sure ain't no student. I'm a chopper pilot—I work on an oil rig over in Mendoza." He motioned toward the mountains to the east. "On the other side of them. Got one more day of paid vacation and I sure as hell ain't going to spend it in that place. A dog don't shit where he eats, right? So, hey, what do you do for a living?"

"Oh . . . I'm an anthropologist."

The bearded boy's eyes lighted up.

"Going to search for Bigfoot up in the Andes?"

Bunch shook his head.

"Going to a conference. The government's sponsoring a colloquium on the Pacific Basin. On Rapa Nui. That's Easter Island to you."

"I been there. All them stone faces, man—you'll fit right in."

Bunch found a cab at the foot of the hill. It wasn't difficult making known his destination to the driver, who knew enough English to help him out.

"Mi esposa," Bunch said, "she teaches Spanish in the United States. She loves the writers Gárcia Márquez and Vargas?"

The driver, a thick-shouldered bald man wearing a leather jacket, nodded at each statement. After traveling for about two blocks the car bucked and sputtered. The driver pulled over to the curb and got out. Bunch turned to see him remove a five-liter tin of gasoline from the trunk and proceed to empty it into the gas tank.

"Problems with gas?" he said when the driver got back behind the steering wheel.

The man shrugged.

"What do you think of the government?" Bunch asked.

The driver glanced at him in the rearview mirror and shook his head.

"It looked pretty normal to me out there," Bunch said, picking up the small fried meat pastry and giving it a sniff. "Empanadas, huh? They smell pretty good."

"It's the national snack," said Yamaguchi. They were sitting in the small, crowded cafeteria at the embassy. It reminded Bunch of the cafeteria in the small California junior college where he had once taught.

"My wife didn't know much about the cuisine," Bunch said. "But she told me a lot about the coup."

"It wasn't really a coup," Yamaguchi said. "It was more like a civil war that lasted only a few days. The impractical idealists on the one side and the unethical pragmatists on the other. With some crossovers on either side, of course. The pragmatists won. They had the army."

"I've . . . read about the torture. Is it still going on?"

Yamaguchi lighted a cigarette and looked around the room. Bunch did the same. You could tell the North American men by the cut of their hair. Otherwise all the men in the room wore the same simple, neatly pressed suits. All the women appeared to be local. He could tell by their oddly beautiful but unfashionable make-up and hairdos.

"The government set up a bureau. It's hard to dismantle a bureaucracy once it gets entrenched. But it's slackening off."

He blew smoke off to one side of the table and then said, "Sounds as though your wife briefed you in depth before you left home."

"Before she left," Bunch said, finding himself smiling again for the second time that day. "I don't know why I said that."

"Tell you," Yamaguchi said, "it happens to us when we're in foreign places. We talk more easily about the things that count."

"She wanted me to boycott the conference," Bunch said. "I . . . couldn't."

"I don't blame you," Yamaguchi said. "We all have our work. I don't like what goes on here, particularly. But what if I refused to serve? What if everybody did?"

"My paper pertains to the Pacific Basin, not to Chile," Bunch said.

"I know. I saw the program. I'd like to read your paper. I read your article in *Scientific American.* You make ethnology really exciting. It makes me want to go back to school and take courses."

"Thanks," said Bunch. "Do you know, I had a graduate student, a friend of ours, who's doing a screenplay based on that article?"

"All those migrating hundreds in long canoes," said Yamaguchi. "I can see it all now. Except I think I did see it. In *Hawaii.* Didn't you see the film of *Hawaii*?

"No," Bunch said, fingering the greasy surface of the empanada on his plate. "I don't go to many movies. I'll have to tell him."

"It was years ago," Yamaguchi said, giving him a curious look.

LAND OF COTTON

Who knows how they had gotten this far from New England? But here they were, traveling down the Shenandoah Valley toward the Nashville that used to be home for them all. Val and Len were in front as usual, with her at the wheel of the Toyota wagon, and, in the back, their children: Weepy, Sneez, and Cheerball—play names from better days. No one was joking now, but the kids tried, blindly, heroically.

"I wish I was in the land of cotton!" sang the eldest. This was Cheerball, James Edison, chanting the song that had captured his eight-year-old imagination at day camp in Vermont. His music teacher had fiddled, and his father had listened and watched—and burned. Burned!

But stop it, Val scolded herself as she stared straight ahead, driving them at sixty-two miles per hour along this valley famous in history and song.

"My feet stink and yours are rotten!"

Now she was the one who burned, and not with desire. And when she heard Wendy, her youngest, squeak in pain, she whirled a hand behind her and struck out.

"It wasn't me," Weepy—Wendy—protested.

"Weepy got a spa-a-an-kin'." This was Sneez, the middle child, a year older than her sister.

"I was just singing," Cheerball said.

"Kids!" Len turned in his seat and tried to stare them down.

The faces of the three children showed blank in Val's rearview mirror. She tried to keep her own emotion from showing, but fire rose to her cheeks like the heat of the late summer Nashville afternoons, the weather to which she had never adjusted.

"Sorry," she said at last. "I know it's not their fault." Val wouldn't look at Len's face, the smoothly shaven cheeks, the red-orange hair curled in the humidity. Lamblike, she had always thought, the hair on his head, the hair on his chest. It gave his body a boyish cast without ever leading you to think that he wasn't a man.

"My fault, of course." Something in Len's voice increased the effect of the heat on her cheeks.

"Are you being ironic again? It's too hot and uncomfortable for being ironic."

"I'm getting that way," he said, a touch of his familiar good humor still present in the way that he moved his hands. He sang quietly, *"My feet stink and yours are rotten. . . ."*

She gripped the wheel so tightly that cramps gripped the palms of her hands, pain laced through her fingers. His old joking, the gentle fun and laughter—all this he was taking away, and she burned, fairly well sizzled. The kids were mewing, nagging, sparring.

"I had to," he said then. "I'm getting old."

"Not here," Val said back, and for miles she chanted, over and over in her mind, "not here, not now, the kids."

But she did talk about it again—how could she suppress it?—when they were sitting at the side of the motel pool. Seven o'clock at night, and the sun still threw off heat like a boiler. New Englanders both, Val and Len had never welcomed the fiercesome climate of this part of the country where they had emigrated to take jobs just after Cheer was born. Every summer since then, just as the days became drenched in such humidity that there might have been a river in the air, they'd head north to the enlarged country cottage Len's father had bought as a retreat from his Boston insurance office.

They'd not been happy, been at ease, those weeks each year in the grand old man's house. Len's father had seen to that. But at least they'd not been hot. When the old man died, Len, an only child, had inherited the place.

That had happened two years ago. At the beginning of this summer Len had loudly, suddenly declared that he had exorcised his father's presence from his life. Val felt her face tighten in a mocking smile. But for that, she might have worried a bit more, watched him more carefully, though what good she might have done she couldn't say.

"I didn't know these things," Len was explaining. "I *couldn't* know these things."

Cheerball, the lone swimmer, paddled about the deep end while the two girls splashed and shouted in the shallows. Len—good father, bad father?—kept an eye on them.

"Weepy!" Sneez's high squeak went up. "I'm telling! Hey!"

"I knew a little," Val said after a while. She was poking a finger at her brown right forearm, poking, poking, watching her flesh ripple.

"How could you know more than I did? And *I* knew nothing."

"Nothing?"

She squinted at him, this lamblike husband of hers, a reddish-brown figure because of the strange effect of the light on this late southern afternoon.

"Nothing. Someone like Michael. . . . What did I know?"

"*He* never made any secret of it."

"Take *that,* Weepy," came Sneez's voice from the water, and Val inched forward in her deck chair, ready to rush to the pool's edge.

Len reached over and closed his hand around Val's.

"What did you know?"

What *did* she know? Fragments he had told her of dreams that only in retrospect appeared somewhat suspect? A certain way of touching? That, too, suspect? Who knew? Who could say? But here they were, talking about it again.

They had agreed that together, without rancor, they would try to conduct the children back home. Home? It was a kind of anti-honeymoon, this trip. Val shook her head. The day had passed in heat and wondering, self-incrimination, and she didn't know how she would survive the night.

"We've got to do it," Val had insisted when Len had come to her with his own plan about meeting them in Nashville and then heading north again. She'd spoken out of selfishness, imagining the trip beforehand, doing it all alone. The kids would be wild—where's Daddy? they'd ask with every pinch at each other's hides—wilder than usual. She wouldn't be able to handle the back-seat chaos and drive, as well.

As it turned out, what chaos the kids failed to achieve she had conjured up herself in her heart. She knew where Len had gone with Michael the last few days before the departure for Nashville, but where was he going now?

"I want to try and get a Vandy student to live in," she said while the children were changing. Fears that she'd fought back all day long while behind the wheel now bobbed up in her mind as kids raced naked about the room, squealing, giggling, as though they still had a family life. Looking at Cheerball, she wanted to let it all go, to cry and cry the way she'd often felt she needed to since Len had told her. But something kept her from it, perhaps the same ambiguous strength—born of repression—that now kept her from wondering about the rest of the night.

"It's not that I won't be around," Len said. He had asked for and gotten an emergency leave from the medical center, the second in two years. The first had been for the death of his father; this one, as he put it, was for the birth of himself.

"Is Michael . . . ?"

"Is he coming down? I don't know. We don't know. He's got his own obligations up there." Len looked away, watched a bare-buttocked girl-child jump up and down on the bed, up and down, before he firmly took her hand and then held her close and stopped the riot. "Just because I found out one thing doesn't make everything else fall into place, you know."

Val stared at him. She had a speech in mind. All those years, the speech began. All those years. . . . But she didn't begin. Instead she urged the children on toward dinner.

"Cheer, Wendy. . . ."

And they walked together to the motel dining room, a large, chilly place where paintings of Civil War officers, Union and Confederate, decorated the walls.

"I always thought doctors were so repressed," she said during the middle of the meal.

"And I thought," Len said, urging their youngest to try her salad, "that we weren't going to talk about such things at times like this."

Val slammed her fork against her plate.

"Violence doesn't help," Len said.

"Why *don't* violets?" Weepy waved her own little fork at Val, Len, Cheer.

"Don't be a dummy," Cheerball said, raising a fist toward her.

"Cheer!" Len grabbed his arm.

"No violets!" Wendy stared at her father's fingers around Cheer's arm, then turned to Val, eyes big, knowing more than she could know.

"You're hurting me!"

"Len . . . ," Val said slowly, tightly, "let the boy go."

"Just watch it." Len drew back his hand. "And sit down."

"I'm leaving," Cheer said to no one, everyone, and straightened his shoulders.

Val looked around at the other diners, some of whom were staring as her oldest child left the room in a wolflike lope between the tables.

Len was rubbing his eyes, his lips tight together. "I'll get him," he said quietly.

Val watched him go, felt something go with them.

Weepy Wendy picked at her salad. "Where they going, Mama?"

"To have a talk," Val said. She felt a hard, rough-edged lump in her chest just above her breastbone, as though one of the children's toys had gotten lodged there. She wanted no more talk with Len—where did talking get them? To this room? To this pass? She wanted to take something like that toy and beat him on the skull, smash him until he moaned and bled.

"I want a talk," Sneez put in, tapping a finger loudly against her milk glass.

"Do you want to knock that over?" Val felt the violets in her voice like straw, saw her hand in the air.

"No," Sneez whispered and began to cry.

"Ma!" Wendy pointed across the room.

Toward them came Len and Cheer, holding hands. It was a peaceable sign—but then Val thought, much to her horror, what if, what if? She shook her head, moving the milk glass across the table toward Sneez as though it were a chesspiece. Nameless commanders (whose faces, at least, she thought she should have known) stared down at her from the walls of the dining room.

The motel room itself gave off the odor of soap and toothpaste, and for the next half hour Val concentrated on the laving of the children, their bodies, their hair, their teeth, while Len, who seemed to understand her need to abrogate their usual arrangement about sharing such labors, lay on one of the beds and read a newspaper. Heat wave, cold front, headlines about temperatures passed before her own eyes and she could feel herself trembling, the worry rising like water up to the rim of a river wall. She and Len had planned—this trip would be like all the other homecomings. The two girls would sleep in the second bed and Cheer would take the rollaway.

"I can't sleep when you're talking," Cheer called over the bodies of his sisters, whispering in their first slumber, when Val again started to raise questions with Len.

"Hush up!" she shushed out.

"Take it easy," Len said, setting down his newspaper only now, although with most of the lights out it had been far too dark to properly read. Val looked him over, this man sitting with his back against the pillow, eyes momentarily shut in thought or fatigue. If she didn't know, he would be the portrait—living sculpture—of a family man at the end of a hard day's drive. But she did—and she felt like a jumper out on a ledge.

"I'll be back in a few minutes," she heard herself say.

"Mom?"

"I'm going for a little walk, Cheer. Daddy's here. You go to sleep."

She could feel the child's eyes, as well as Len's, follow her to the door. Their stares seemed to project all the heat and anger and puzzlement of the day. For a moment she hesitated—why try to run? But then something beyond her doing propelled her into the hot soup of the southern night. Cars stood in even rows, like metal loaves baking in the dark; moths fluttered around the tall parking lot lamps, upward falling snow, and the rumbling, rumbling of the air conditioners attached to the walls of each room made a thundering music. Val felt herself stewing in the night kitchen. There should have been a huge storm gathering across the fields that separated the lot from the highway, but from that direction Val detected no sound—if there was sound it had died under the roar of the motel's noises—and she saw nothing but blackness, zero.

She took a few turns around the swimming pool in the hotel's inner courtyard and got as much satisfaction as she could find on the premises: her wavery reflection upon the light-splashed water. Should she do the bar? Sit until a passing salesman, tepid in his sweat-stained shirt in the midst of the air-conditioned chamber, asked her to his bed? Should she dump all, just jump in the car and drive? If she could just get through tonight. . . . She resigned herself, fists clenched, to living the next years as part of a mystery in which she would be merely a player.

"Feeling okay?" Len looked up from the paperback he had been reading. He was still sprawled on top of the turned-down cover of the bed.

Val strained to see the title, but the light was no better now than it had been when she had left, and he had, in any case, slipped the book over the side and onto the far floor.

"I'm feeling that I'm not feeling," Val said, turning to attend to the bare-limbed children whose bodies he might have covered before her return but had not.

"Sorry that we're doing it this way?"

"I suppose. . . ." Tugging at legs and arms and sheets, she could feel something, a choking wave of irritating heat.

"It's been all right for them," Len said. "If we hadn't done it this way, imagine. . . ."

"Yes," she said, suddenly needing to cover her face with her hands, as though her entire visage were made of some fragile, cracked material. Then she was in the bathroom. She washed and wept, wept and washed. Minutes passed. He was holding the book up again when she came out.

"What's that?" she asked.

"Nothing important."

"*That* stuff?"

"What stuff?"

"You know."

"Oh, Val . . ." He set the book aside, this time near the lamp on the bedside table, and held out his hands to her. "I *do* still love you," he said, his hands motionless before him.

In the dark pool of air-conditioned chill she shivered as though summer had abruptly changed to winter. She climbed into the bed. His hands upon her reminded her of things shuffling across some mossy bank of beach, but then finally he kissed her and did not stop. She felt the old tide come upon her. She eased herself onto his hips; they were pieces of a puzzle moving together in the dark.

"Goodbye," he said.

Her head jerked back, as though he had clipped her on the chin. She rolled to one side, like a child dismounting from a ride in some amusement park, feeling the sudden pressure of darkness, not just in the room, but beyond the lamps of the parking lot, beyond and above Virginia, the cold season stretching out to all points west and south, up and down. A child sobbed, and she rocked it—she rocked.

NIGHTS ON THE
CUMBERLAND PLATEAU

Arrival

Your discovery of the plateau may surprise you. Who in the North, or anywhere outside these parts, has heard of it? Geographers? Geologists? Perusers of travel essays in large Sunday supplements? You're rolling through the valley of the Tennessee when suddenly the road turns upward and you're climbing, climbing between a parfait of ancient stone, the last vestiges of the old Appalachians, their westernmost thrust.

After Boston, the weather seems milk-toast mild, green weeds flourishing in the fields alongside the road. Is my own life still green after Jurassic divorce? Here I have come from New England for southern respite, a particular variety of historian with a shattered past.

Welcome

The dean, a clean-shaven fellow young enough to be my son in sports coat and blue jeans, welcomes me officially to my visiting post.

"We ah ver-y guh-lad that you ah he-ah!"

And from his desk—forgive him, for he knows not what he does—he extracts a bottle of what turns out to be an obscure but thoroughly delicious bourbon, glasses, and, from his handy little office refrigerator, ice.

Home?

I've been staying with friends, in attic rooms and small cottages behind main houses, for five, six months now. Or seven, is it? Time runs on. Here I'm given a small, single-structure apartmentlike place in the woods; it's walking distance from my office. Friends—if I had any up here at this elevation—can now visit me.

Watch this—a man unpacks, stretches out on his new bed, missing his old life, his children (though they're mostly grown), the way amputees are reported to miss their absent limbs. You feel their presence—and look down to see that they're gone.

The Drop

Just down the road from my little house lies the Drop, a precipice famous on the plateau. By day you stare off toward a horizon that stretches, you have the illusion, nearly to Memphis. Small, neat squares of farmland spread out below where the wooded coves yield to valley floor. Here, sometimes lower than the man who watches, hawks soar. From this height I notice—by its apparent absence—the precipitate passage of time in the form of slurry cloud and changing light. No wind, except what the hawks appear to draw up from the earth by the magnetism of their outspread wings.

Night

A godly tall actor flings his cape from a great height; darkness falls across the Plateau. Through the rents in the cloth, stars appear. I see them as I stand in the clearing behind my little house. Woods before me, the small light in the window gives me some hope, swaying as I am, weak tree in the wind. I can hear the Drop calling to me: come and look now, it says. Come and look *now!*

Days

The folks are right friendly here, inviting me to lunches and teas. Students clog my office. In class we wear academic gowns, and the atmosphere drips seriousness. Everything goes along well—and then a girl raises her voice in a certain way, or a dog barks outside the classroom window, a car starts, and I'm undone.

Night

Come and look now. Come and look *now*.

The Weather of the Past

My expertise lies in unearthing small, distinctive facts about the weather of the past. In my current state I neglected to add this important note. This morning I woke up to find a thin film of ice on the window of my bedroom and my breath flowed steamy from my yawning mouth. Outside, ice covered the walkways.

Sitting here in my office, the door shut, my feet up on the desk, notebook in hand, I have to admit that southern winters are no worse than arguments with your children or the anger you feel at a misbehaving dog or cat. By ten o'clock the ice is gone, and I can see grass again, no more wilted than it appears in New England after a hot August afternoon sun has beaten it down, when you sit in what passes for shade, drink in hand, wishing for the season to change.

I hear these voices: a woman I met at a party who becomes everything to me, the children we spawn, unthinking, who now grow as I grew, their being no accident to them. I hear these voices only in memory—few of them speak to me now.

Plateau

At sunset head for the Drop. Some afternoons there's a crowd. I meet some of my would-be history students and politely smile, forgetting their names. The disappearance of the suddenly inflamed ball of the descending star does something that never happens with *my* children: it silences them utterly for five full minutes.

Bait

"I saw you at the Drop," said one of the girls in the history class, a busty blonde with sad, searching eyes—a huntress.

I try to make innocuous conversation, but I'm no good at talk with human beings—not live ones. Gee-Gee always spoke for me, and told me that on a number of occasions. I'm no good with human beings, only shards and fossils of small creatures and water lines. But I do talk *to* myself. Don't play with the children, my inner voice tells me while I stare at this student's chest. Don't play with the children.

The Weather of the Past

"I think you should see a doctor," Gee-Gee says.

"And why is that?" I say.

"Why is that? Because you're sick, that's why."

"Well, judge not, lest ye be judged. Bitch."

"See what I mean?"

"What do you mean, see what I mean? You and your goddamn code. You and your nuances. You think you can live your life that way, raising your eyebrows and planting your hand on your elbow? For Christ's sake!"

"And you don't have your own code, do you?"

"Code, sure I have my code. And right now I'm sending out Morse signals—help, S.O.S., Mayday."

"Out!"

"What do you mean, out? This is my house."

"Not any more, buster. Mister Famous Scientist! Out right now! You don't care about me. You don't care about the kids. All you care about is your famous work!"

"And my bugs, don't forget that. And my lizards."

"I don't give a shit about your bugs and your lizards. They're a higher form of life than you are, you creep, and I'd even rather have them around than you."

Going to Nashville

I hear about the lecture at Vanderbilt and drive down the mountain, head west, tracked by a light snowfall. The road signs amuse me. Coffee County. Tullahoma. Stones River. Murfreesboro. Limestone, more limestone. Here is the plateau played out, nothing but airy rock and caves, old river courses.

Remember a cave? We sat under the lip, dark weather, the water drip-dripping, drip-dripping, earth rhythms, earth tone. We were hungry and cold, but we had each other, had each other, until I stepped out on you, or you on me—which one, that's blurred. The days went by; I can't remember. And now the fire's gone out, the children are crying, and I'm sitting in my home, alone.

These thoughts I'm daydreaming to myself during the lecture by this tall, thin, frizz-haired woman, a scholar attached to the Country Music Hall of Fame, an ethno-musicologist from Michigan.

"Oh, you're *you!*" she says when I introduce myself after the talk. "I've read your book, your essays!"

My heart heals up. Simple man that I am, our life together flashes before me, the consummation, the bond formed, the house, new children (it's late in life, we run tests, take precautions), their raising, our late middle-age. . . .

"Of course I'll have a drink," she says in this rose-lit version of my evening. "I've been so"—and she leans closer, tall enough to speak directly into my ear— "lonely down here."

I'm inventing this, of course. I do introduce myself and suggest a drink. But she's tired, though when I mentioned the title of my last book, her eyes showed some dim light of recognition in the midst of sincere fatigue.

"You're staying down here?"

"I commute to Ann Arbor," she says. "My husband's up there in the English department." The light goes out in her eyes. "I'm just on loan to the museum. And you're on the plateau for the semester? How can you stand it? I read an article about it somewhere—it's supposed to be quaint. They wear academic gowns, don't they? But it must be quite isolated. Is your wife with you?"

I shake my head.

"You ought to come and give a lecture and see the place," I say. "Nothing like it anywhere."

"That was my impression. Well . . . see about an honorarium and we'll talk. But would they like to hear about the blues?"

The Weather of the Past

I read that article, too. The dean's secretary had, in fact, handed it to me upon my arrival along with several books, privately printed, by writers who had lived up here in the past. From the striated layers of ancient rock to the American dons and their acolytes in dark, flowing academic robes, the place itself is a plot outside of modern time. What with their processions to and from class and the sculptured towers, replicas of Oxford and Cambridge, the town might have been a movie set, except for the modern automobiles on the street.

Sometimes I don't know whether I am in a small British village with a southern drawl or a southern hamlet with a British accent. Whatever, the place makes me welcome, and its uniqueness both assuages and exacerbates my inner turmoil.

I enjoy listening to the southern speech from every state of the former Confederacy converging here on the mountain on the lips of dozens of my students. At night, to stop myself from eavesdropping on other voices, I invite them over for long conversations about things that mean much to them.

"Do you think—," one of them is asking even now over a glass of California red about ten o'clock on a weekday evening while others sit silently on the floor of my house in the woods, "do you think that God knows all times and places before they occur, or simply as and that they will occur?"

The Drop
Come and look, etc.
   Present
Fog and bird cries at sunup. Outside the air's as mild as Boston in June. Winter appears to be over. What a life they lead here! I work at my desk, shuffling notes about here and there, then and now. But who can find the sanity to write about the quality of darkness of evenings ten thousand years old? Yet some things remain constant—the call of the Drop. That voice comes out of the deep night as ancient as the mind, as young as the conscience. But I'm not hearing that now, not listening. While sitting on my stoop I see a trio of pileated woodpeckers flash past on huge wing and red feather. Whose woods these are.

"I read your book."

The blonde student, the huntress, appears at my doorstep, her eyes alert to my every move.

"That's nice," I say. "I'm flattered."

"I found a copy in the library."

"Lucky. Good library."

"Are you writing a new one?"

I see without turning the notes in disarray on my makeshift desk; I recall dimly the passion for an idea I'd carried with me to these high places.

"Yes, sort of. I'm just in the early stages."

"I'd love to read that one, too," she says, every part of her perfectly still, even her eyes, except that her lips . . . her lips tremble. From the woods birdcall and rustle of brush and branch in the dissipating fog. "I love history."

Nature

It's not that I want to remain disengaged. But there's always a voice, inner or outer, saying stay back or jump off or run now, now, race away. All right for me. But then I married Gee-Gee and fathered some children. Sins of the husbands visited even unto the same generation. I wanted nothing but to do my work—and disengaged myself from Gee-Gee and the kids. And now I'm here. And can't work.

Music City

All Tennessee, like Gaul, is divided into three parts: East, Middle, and West. And in the middle of Middle Tennessee sits Nashville, of which Vanderbilt comprises only one part. What did I know when I attended that lecture? Here's the history man, driving around in the city's nether regions, parking his car in the lot behind a club called Come As You Are. He slinks in for a quick drink, a glimpse of some huge, trembling breasts. Then off to a nearby honky-tonk where a white kid with hair down his shoulders twangs and thrums music that in these parts could be placed under glass in a museum. After thinking in cowardly fashion about buying a woman, he finds himself back in his car, and after contemplating the lonely drive back to the plateau, he finds a motel. Near Vanderbilt. The coward.

"It's me," he says into the telephone in his hand.

"Are you in another zone?" she asks. "It's awfully late here."

"I'm in Nashville," he says.

"So is my husband. Just your luck—and mine, I should say—that he's in the bathroom right this second."

"Sorry. It's about the—"

"Call me at my office," she says and hangs up.

I'd been going to tell her that we did want to hear about her subject.

The Origin of the Blues

These enfolded mountains, detritus of old oceans—picture a Sunday at the beach a hundred million years ago, amphibians beneath their rented umbrellas squinting at the hot young sun, gill-breathing no more but longing for their old mother—by the sea, by the sea, by the beautiful sea—and with their webbed paws clinging to each other in the night—you and me, you and me, oh, how happy we'll be! They listen to the melody and percussion of wind and surf. Reptilian tongues slithery upon each other in the dark. Hours pass. What's time against the pressure of scaly lust? Eons later, day breaks over the dunes and they smile snaky smiles as they greet the light, remembering, remembering, their scales glittering like embroidered garments of coin in the fresh dawn. Here one of my ancestors makes a print where waves whip the shore—and on my walk at daybreak atop the plateau I notice it, after blowing away the shrouds of chipped rock, the very tidal mark where this rendezvous between old sea and new earth took place.

Present

"I am very glad that you invited her here!" says the dean with outstretched hand. "Our students needed to hear the news she brought!"

"I just love music," the huntress interjects, and she smiles at the dean and he smiles at her and they walk off together, arm in arm, toward the circle of students surrounding the frizz-haired ethnologist from the North Coast.

In the morning fog, with the first crocuses pushing up through the water-soaked ground, her hair stands out as though she's been electrified.

"That's true, in a way," she says when I tell her.

"Thank you," I say, not knowing what else to do.

" 'Thank you,' the man says. The man says, 'thank you.' " And she laughs, the covers slip down to her waist, and I see in clear morning light her slender neck and chest, freckled, like a young girl's.

"You remind me of a colt," I say.

"Thank you," she says, throwing her arms around me.

" 'Thank you,' the woman says," I say in her ear. " 'Thank you.' "

Eventually, we get out of bed, shower, dress. She's got her drive back to Nashville, and a trip to Michigan on the weekend. I've got pages to write, students to see. We know each other's numbers, but we make no plans. Outside, an April morning, warm as Boston in June.

The Drop

There's something about the school year that encourages the optimist, even when he's down. If we began in spring and ended in winter, oh, and how the heart would grow heavy. But our scenario commences in autumn, in the dying season, and moves through the shortest days and darkest nights toward a time of rejuvenation. This allows the likes of me to ponder the most troubling of cycles, ends of eons, the death of entire species of beast and fish and bird, the eventual demise of the planet.

Come and look, the edge of the universe calls out to me. Come and see what I can do—and will. But here I sit, happy as a swatch of lichen, looking out over the sunlit abyss, the space between this cliff and the valley, while hawks hover beneath my feet, and the clouds sail by, as they did past lizards and monkeys, and as they will pass the angels without wings who may one lucky day replace the kind of man I have become.

THE SEALS

Burr was standing precariously on the downward slope, watering the apricot trees shaken aslant in the last earth tremor, when he heard the horn bark from the top of the hill. He set down the hose and climbed the rough wooden steps and opened the door hanging crooked on its hinges in the fence, surprised to find himself suddenly imagining—a frequent fear at night in the house alone, but not ever before now under a brilliant afternoon sun—that he was an intruder and had just discovered the back way onto the patio of the red-shingled old ranch-style house. He hurried through the house to greet his guests, a tanned blond woman his own age with a slender body and a weathered face and a girl about eighteen with a similar complexion but much fuller body pulling new, hunter-green suitcases from the trunk of a blue rental sedan.

"Hey, Sally, Tish, welcome." He tried to take a suitcase from the girl, but she fought him off.

"I can handle it," she said, and Burr noticed something pass across her face, as if she'd just suffered a recent injury in one of the numerous sports she practiced and was bullying on with her life as her late grandfather, his father-in-law, had always urged them, injured, depressed, whatever, to do.

"You were such a dear to invite us," Sally, his sister-in-law said, striking at his cheek with her lips as she allowed him to take a suitcase from her hand.

"I'm glad somebody needs my help," Burr said, showing his pleasure at their arrival with the biggest smile he'd produced in months. He had only recently admitted to himself how lonely he had been, house-sitting here for a friend who had gone east for the summer; so when Sally had called the week before to say that she and her daughter were coming to California (for what she called "some business" at Stanford), he had invited them to stay for a few days here in Santa Cruz. The kind of work he did—creating brochures for various philanthropic organizations, with a sanitorium or retirement village thrown in now and then to vary the pot—made his week flexible enough to take time off for his visitors. And, besides, after several months without a word from his wife, he could be sure that he would hear something about Buffy from her older (and always more sensible) sister.

A few minutes later, on the patio, he had the time to take a good look at this woman and her daughter, neither of whom he had seen since he and Buffy had moved west in a drastic attempt to save their marriage. Sally was nearly fifty now, but still as trim as when he had first met her, at the Japanese pavilion at the World's Fair in Flushing, when Buffy had decided that it was time for him to meet the family, all of whom were coming up for the event from Florida. It was now how many years later? He did a little computation in his head but lost track of it in the middle, noticing how close a resemblance his niece made to the way Buffy had looked when they had first met—that date, he knew, Fourth of July, 1962, Riverside Park. That had been close to the beginning of what he thought of as his real life. Here on this patio, behind the red-shingled house he had moved to when Buffy had told him that she didn't want him around anymore, beneath the sheet of nearly translucent blue sky beyond the eucalyptus that towered above all the other trees on the torn and downward slope, he believed that he was close to the end.

"Mother," Tish said with a slight drawl. She uncrossed her legs and stood up. "I've got to—"

"I know, darling," Sally said. "Burr, we'll unpack now, if you like."

That was the family manner, to sweep you up in the off-hand way in which they allowed you to be hospitable to them. Burr had wanted to ask questions but put it off, leading mother and daughter back into the house, through the kitchen and the large living room with its stone fireplace and television monitor and into the bedroom where he had been sleeping alone in the king-size bed, fearful almost every night of unrealized mayhem and disaster.

"If you don't mind sharing this," he said to Sally.

"We're real close," Tish said, and Burr couldn't tell if she was being sincere or ironic or something other.

"It should be comfortable. A good mattress." Burr patted it, feeling suddenly a little embarrassed, playing motel clerk.

"And you're sleeping . . . ?"

Sally looked concerned.

"In the study. There's a single bed in there where I work. So, hey, I've got great plans for us, dinner tonight at a terrific Indian place downtown, and tomorrow a little drive up the coast. . . ."

"Anything you want to do will be just *fi-i-ine,*" Sally said, her voice a replica of the lost Buffy's, whose name none of them had as yet even spoken. She flashed him a smile and closed the door behind her.

Burr stood for a moment at the door listening to the muffled conversation within and then walked back through the house and out onto the patio, where he stared at the sky, a broad smear of pure blue above the eucalyptus: not a hint of the daily fog that draped over the hill in the morning, not a hint of the deep velvet pinpricked by stars that vaulted above the house at night. At this time of day, as on most days at this time in most seasons in this state he had lately adopted as his own, every object within the range of his vision gave off a glow that only stars at night in the east could achieve. He was wondering at this and staring down the slope at the fruit trees when he remembered with a start that he had not turned off the spigot and so was allowing precious water to run, wasted, down the hillside into the little creek at the property line. He walked quickly toward the far side of the house, which took him directly past the floor-to-ceiling windows of the living room and then the master bedroom. A glance within showed him mother and daughter, clinging to each other in the center of the room, a two-headed, two-backed, long-legged blond animal of gently sloping shoulders and beautifully molded calves.

A ride along the ocean just at sunset, a stop to watch the surfers pushed in on the curls like dead black leaves driven before a windstorm, Burr behind the wheel, Sally beside him, Tish in the back: it was enough like a family outing, or the ghost of one, to give him a sickly fear of never coming out of this funk he had fallen into when Buffy called that afternoon and said that she was leaving for Europe. He urged them to get out of the car—a good host would want to do that—but he was sorry he did because standing on the bluff overlooking the rocks and the silvery, undulating ocean he felt as though he were falling and the only thing that kept him upright was a wind straight from China. He'd been feeling a lot of these things over the past few months, the worry of intruders, memory lapses (the hose, the spigot), desperate solitude. But now, glancing at the two women standing alongside him, their lips curled back against the rush of air, he saw so much of his wife's face in Sally's, so much of what he wanted in Tish's body, that he pictured the night to come with an animal anticipation that shocked him, not with its crudity, but because of the warm flow of pleasure flushing through his chest.

Dinner heated him up even more, and he drank wine to cool his mouth and throat.

"You?" he said, noticing that Sally had left her wine untouched.

"I shouldn't," she said. "That's what I do when Ken is away on a job and it gets me into nothing but trouble."

"Trouble?"

"Oh, you know, with him, when he gets home; I want to taper off and he wants me to keep up with him."

"You don't drink?" he said to his niece, who sat across from him dabbing at her rice with a fork.

"Can't, Uncle Burr, I'm on medication."

"Maybe I *will*," Sally said, distracting Burr with white teeth he'd seen only before in the mouth of his absent wife. Even Tish could not produce a smile so brilliant, he had noticed, he realized now, when they had spoken.

"I deserve this drink," Sally said.

"Oh, Mother, please," Tish said.

"I do," Sally said.

"Sure you do," Tish said.

"Burr," Sally said, "has Buffy written to you at all since she left?"

"Oh great, Mom," Tish said.

"No, no, he's been meaning to ask me things, I know," Sally said.

"No," Burr said, chewing on some food.

"What a bitch," Tish said.

"Tish!"

"That's what she is, now that we're talking about it, Mama."

"I don't think we ought to spend the evening running Buffy into the ground," Burr said, swallowing hard.

"I guess you have the right to say that, Burr," Sally said.

"She's still a bitch," Tish said. "When—"

"Hey, enough," Sally said. "Cut the gloom, hey?"

Tish, with her otherwise pretty lips, made a schoolgirl sneer.

"Gee, if Daddy were here he could say, 'Here's a knife, now cut the gloom.' Except, Mom, don't you think that this gloom would bend the knife?"

Sally took another swallow of wine.

"Sally?" Tish said.

"I am your mother," Sally said. "Please don't call me by my name."

Burr suggested that they drive to the yacht club for a drink after dinner, but Tish complained that she was tired, and Sally said that they had to get her home to bed. On the way, Burr thought of renting a movie, and Sally said that would be fine, and he stopped at the video store and came out to ask if either of them had seen *Broadway Danny Rose*.

"Did that play in Houston?" Sally said.

"It did, Mom," Tish said.

"But you haven't seen it, have you?" Burr asked from outside the car.

"Rent it, Uncle Burr," his niece said. "Hey, where's that place you're taking us tomorrow?"

"Surprise," he said.

"Oh, I've been *there*. My parents used to take me *there* when I was little. I'm going again soon."

"Tomorrow," Burr said.

"No, not tomorrow, Uncle Burr. But soon."

"*Tish,*" Sally said in a voice he had never heard her use before, but a voice he had heard in Buffy's throat.

"*Sally,*" Tish said, in a voice equally strange and equally familiar.

"I am your mother," Sally said, nothing more. When Burr pulled into the gravel driveway before the red-shingled house on the bluff, she got out of the car and went inside and into the bathroom in the hall. Tish headed into the bedroom and came out a few moments later, surprising Burr where he was hovering over the VCR. Her tan legs were bare and she wore a T-shirt stretched across her chest on which was inscribed in red letters

LIFE'S A BITCH
FIRST YOU SUFFER AND
THEN YOU DIE

"Your mother's not going to like that," he said, standing to face her.

"How do you know?" She sounded suddenly groggy, as though she had been drinking more than either of the two older people. "It's a joke. She's big on cutting the gloom."

Sally, in fact, was silent when in the next moment she entered the room and saw them standing before the screen. Tish rose on tiptoe and dutifully kissed her uncle on the cheek. Marvelously fresh odors from her hair and skin made Burr step back and savor what he had just inhaled, while the girl murmured something to her mother and left the room.

"Shall we watch?" Sally said, her eyes a bit unfocused, filmed over nearly, as though she had already just watched a movie while fighting off sleep instead of waiting to see one.

Burr pushed the buttons, sat in a chair near the one where Sally had seated herself. After a few minutes she asked him to pause the film and she went into the bedroom and came out wearing a green Chinese-style robe. Burr started the movie again. She asked for a glass of red wine. Burr paused the film and poured some for both of them. About half an hour later a faint cry went up in another part of the house and Sally raced from the room. Burr paused the film.

"My little girl," she said when she returned. "A nightmare. I think the medicine has something to do with it."

"What's she taking?" Burr asked. His hand was poised above the remote control unit on the arm of his chair.

"You don't want to know," Sally said, her eyes wandering from the image on the screen to his face and back again.

"There are some things I want to know," Burr said. "I want to know about Buffy."

"My sister," Sally said, slurring her words slightly. "Awful thing to know."

"Is that right?"

"I know it sounds mean, but the world is mean."

"Mean?" He pushed the button to start the film again.

"Mean."

Burr watched the images on the monitor, a fight, a chase through a large empty warehouse. He sipped his wine, and when he looked up Sally was standing next to his chair.

Morning—and they found themselves driving up the coast road past the cement plant at Davenport, past fields of brussels sprouts and artichoke plants that carpeted the way between the highway and the sparkling sea. A line of fog, retreating early from the shoreline, made the horizon a cottony streak far out upon the water. Burr had shaved, cursorily, and had splashed on some cologne. Mother and daughter wore jeans and running shoes, ready for a little hike. Despite her long sleep, Tish seemed less rested than Sally, who had been up most of the night.

"Are you all right?" Burr said, speaking to her with his eyes on the rearview mirror.

"Me?" Tish stared back at him the same way.

"I told him something," Sally said, turning in her seat as if she could not get comfortable.

"Mother. . . ." The word escaped the girl's lips like gas from a deflating balloon.

"This stuff you're going to try at Stanford tomorrow," Burr said.

"Mother," Tish said, "can't I even speak a little about my own disease?"

"Speak," her mother said.

"Thanks, much," Tish said. "They called our doctor at home about two weeks ago, Uncle Burr. They told us to come out right away because they want to try something on me."

"Some new procedure," Sally said.

"*Sally,*" Tish said.

"Okay, okay, don't call me that, okay?"

"Some new procedure," Burr said, staring at the road ahead, the fertile strips of farmland stretching to the cliffs above the steaming surf. "What is it?"

"It's a surprise," Tish said.

"She knows all about it," Sally said.

"I don't really want to know," Tish said, catching Burr's eye in the mirror.

He held her gaze, then paused and looked away to the ocean and sky to the west, thinking he had forgotten something, not the spigot this time, something else, something different; but he made himself concentrate on the little distance they had left as they approached the high, mud-red cliffs where the tree-lined mountains sheared off at the sea.

"Does Buffy know about this?" he asked.

"Daddy doesn't even know," Tish said.

"You're kidding," Burr said, checking the cliffs as they rushed past. Rocks loosened in rainstorms sometimes rolled down onto the highway, boulders even. People had been killed.

"He's been away for months," Sally said.

"The oilman's away, but life goes on—or death," Tish said.

"Aren't you cute?" Sally said, turning to try and look into her daughter's face.

"It's the truth. If you had wanted Daddy to come home and be with us you would have written him about it."

"I didn't want to alarm him," Sally said.

"You didn't want him back," Tish said.

"I can handle this alone," Sally said.

"What about me?" Tish said.

"Ladies. . . ." Burr clenched the wheel hard, slowing for a turn onto a paved road off to the left at a sign saying "Año Nuevo State Reserve."

"*You* want Kendrick back?" Sally said and laughed.

"I want someone, too," Tish said.

"Now *what* do you mean by that?" her mother said.

"You know what I mean, Sally," Tish said.

They drove slowly beyond the park ranger's booth and stopped in a sandy area bordered with tarry timbers. The horizon turned white where the dunes rose to hide the breakers, but all the fog had disappeared.

"I've been thinking about coming here for months now," Burr said as they put the car behind them and struck out on a barely discernible path through the ice plants and other seaside scrub. "You two are a good excuse."

"For what, I wish you'd tell me," Tish said, and headed off out along an obviously less-traveled route that veered southward toward the higher dunes.

"Don't get lost," her mother called to her as she and Burr walked further in a westerly direction. The sun had eased around in the sky almost directly above Tish, giving off waves of much-desired warmth as they pushed forward into the wind from the ocean ahead.

Burr, walking just a foot or so ahead of his sister-in-law, said, "What are . . . her chances?"

"God, Burr, I don't want to talk about it," Sally said, staring at the dunes ahead of them. From somewhere in that direction came now a faint howling and intermittent barks punctuated by the crashing of the surf, as though all the dogs in the county might be gathering there to meet them.

"I'm pregnant and I don't know what the Christ to do."

"Well," Burr said, "is it Kendrick's? You said he's been away."

"He's been away all right. I don't know if it's his. I didn't go looking for it. I didn't know anything about Tish's condition when this happened—that came so sudden, or this did—but maybe I'm psychic, what do you think? That I'm going to lose one baby, so I've got another coming?"

They had reached the edge of a small rise and threaded their way carefully down a narrow cut in the sand. The barking ahead of them turned to a hoarse trumpeting, a sporadic burst of sound that mingled with the low roar of the surf.

"The experimental thing at Stanford, that'll save your old baby," Burr said, looking down at the cove that came into view, its beach layered with boulders and large rounded masses of animals up from the sea. Birds swooped low off the water, flying in from nowhere, their voices squalling above the barks and roars.

Sally used both hands to hold his arm, as though he might, without her as ballast—or she might, without him—float off the beach into the undulating wall of light and surf and sound.

"I don't think it's going to save her," she said. "The doctor doesn't even think so."

"So you're going to keep this new child?"

"Uh-huh," Sally made a noise. "Even if it looks like one of those," she said, staring off at one of the monstrously ugly beasts that slept in the sun only a few yards ahead on the sand. "You want to hear now about that wayward wife of yours, my sister?"

Burr shook his head.

"I can wait," he said, spying Tish walking out from behind a clump of reed and sea grass to point, with a clean motion of her finger and hand, at two young elephant seal bulls splashing about in the surf, playing or fighting—it couldn't be said clearly which, at least not by an ignorant observer. Towering grey-black creatures with glistening hides and teeth like fence pickets sticking from their hideous elongated snouts, they shrieked and lunged and butted and slashed each other under a morning sun that lit the scene with the odd intensity of a fire in space.

Burr felt his knees give a little, as though the tremor, or the murder he had been fearing would come in the middle of the night, had caught him under the bright light of an ordinary day. He turned abruptly from the signifying girl at the waterline, and from her mother, too, believing he was safe now from the meaning he feared had nearly burst upon him. He took a few faltering steps back toward the path, and that was when he saw it: a huge, mottled elephant seal cow raising its nightmare head from among the reeds and, seeing him for a second or two, meeting his eye. Whose look was emptier, the waking beast's or his?